Hi.

In case you're wondering, it all started a long, long time ago, while I was still in school

I was sharpening my quill pen, after having chased our quill supplier - a half bald chicken - all over the school yard, when my teacher yelled: "Cicale! You call this stuff a comprehensive dissertation on the bubonic plague? Don't make me laugh."

So I figured, hey, only someone really sick and deeply disturbed and totally deranged could make The Black Death sound funny. Obviously, I had all the qualifications to be a humor writer - or, perhaps, a candidate for the happy farm. Same thing, I guess.

Either way, I know that Shakespeare would have been proud that he and I had been expelled from separate schools together. Just think, if only he had persevered, he too could have been published in The Hanford Sentinel…

Much of the canine and spousal craziness in this book is the result of excessive exposure to the alarming vicissitudes of Shirlee and Fifi, without whom... Anyway, it's their own fault for being so strange.

I'M BEING HUGGED

IN ALL THE WRONG PLACES

Cover art and graphics by Lawrence Heinze

Cover design by Julie Sartain

'Baseball bat' and 'old car' graphics by Anthony Cicale

I'M BEING HUGGED

IN ALL THE WRONG PLACES

Anthony Cicale

Here are 46 of the 500 humor columns written by Anthony Cicale and published in The Hanford Sentinel over the past years under the title *A Pinch Of Salt.*

At the time of going to press, Anthony Cicale is still writing a humor column, which appears every Sunday in that newspaper. All three of his readers are sometimes pleased about this, although, they don't like anyone to know.

Anthony Cicale has also written for the San Francisco Examiner and the Fresno Bee and published amusing interviews with many famous music stars together with reviews of their performances. There is some dispute about whether these interviews were really supposed to be amusing. If you are feeling brave, perhaps you should ask the music stars what they think.

CONTENTS

1. LOOK, I'M ALREADY BEING HUGGED

Now don't get me wrong, I have nothing against hugging. I like to be hugged. Some of my best friends are huggers. But don't you think hugging is getting out of control? Everyone's doing it, everywhere, all the time.

The very first huggers wanted everyone to feel loved. It was just a wonderful Sunday morning thing; but now, like an unstoppable epidemic, hugging has embraced every level of society.

Football players, who used to pat each other's bottoms, now hug instead. Some have shown a disturbing tendency to do both at the same time. Do they just like each other more than they used to? Where will it all end?

The point is that some perfectly normal people, who deserve to be loved, have an aversion to hugging. Afraid to encourage it they are forced to sneak around with eyes lowered and arms folded defensively across their chest. They hope this will be interpreted as "look, I'm already being hugged," or, "look, I'm having a heart attack." This may prevent hugging but you should watch out for mouth-to-mouth resuscitation.

Strangers in a Supermarket will suddenly throw themselves into each other's arms. As you all know there is usually plenty of time for this kind of thing in the high speed, Express Checkout Line. And once you've hugged, you will be expected to hug every time you meet.

One of the difficult aspects of hugging a stranger is knowing how hard to hug. If you don't squeeze hard enough it implies that you don't really want to hug at all. So you squeeze a little harder and take your cue from your partner.

But if your partner is taking his cue from you, he will squeeze still harder, and soon one of you will faint from lack of oxygen. Usually this will result in sidelong glances from nearby undecided huggers, hurriedly folding their arms across their chest.

The important thing to remember when hugging is to pat your partner on the back the whole time. This is a signal that it's platonic. Just keep patting – especially if your partner is not patting.

Sometimes you can spot someone who prefers not to be hugged. The signs are subtle and you could easily miss them. One easy to miss sign is a suit of armor covered in poisonous six-inch spikes. But, many huggers are not so easily put off.

Like most nice things, hugging is good in moderation. But, these days you could go to a friend's house for dinner and be greeted at the door by your hosts and ten other guests. This is a sign that you will all become close friends before you are actually allowed near any food.

So you hug his wife and he hugs your wife and then you hug her husband and his wife hugs your wife. And everyone's keeping an eye out for anyone who isn't patting his partner's back.

After this, you and the ten other guests will begin to hug each other. And, after a while no one cares if you are patting or not, all they want is dinner; and, remember, whenever you meet any of them again you will be expected... Well, I've told you all that already.

Even our dog, Fifi, who picks things up quickly, has started to hug people's legs, and she sometimes does it when we are trying to hurry guests who have stayed too long. It gives a whole new meaning to the term, "shake a leg," I can tell you.

There are some hugging rules you will be well advised to respect. If you don't hug someone at church on Sunday, it's antisocial. But if you do hug someone at the office on Monday it's harassment. Well, don't blame me. I didn't make the rules.

Even heads of state have replaced the handshake with the hug. It began a while ago when President Clinton hugged Yasir Arafat. There is a rumor that during the presidential clinch, Hillary, seeing that Arafat was wearing a very becoming dress, hissed urgently into his ear, "Pat his back, Yasir, for heaven's sake, pat his back." Yasir probably took her advice because Bill never invited him back.

Now I can only hope my two remaining friends will understand that, although I'm not an addict I still like to be hugged sometimes. Just remember: if Fifi hugs your leg, pat her back, okay?

2. HAPPINESS IS A WAGGING TAIL

Dogs are not really dumb, you know. They can't speak but they express themselves clearly and with more of a flourish than we do. When a dog is happy it wags its tail, right? Not only is the meaning clear, it has the virtue of silence.

Ok, you're right; we humans can smile and laugh at each other's remarks or guffaw at the boss's joke – even if it's a rotten joke. This is because we have a great capacity for deception.

A dog can't do this. It can't force its tail to wag if it's unhappy. There is just no deception connection. Ok, go on, tell your dog the joke your boss told you. He's not laughing, is he?

He's baring his teeth and his tail is rigid and trembling. There is no doubt about his opinion or what he will do when your boss says, "stop me if you've heard this."

We are forced to look directly at each other to know if we are happy or not. There isn't anything we can do to express our opinion to someone standing behind us – well, hardly anything - and certainly not to the boss. Compared to a dog our ability to communicate is dull and limited.

There is something mysterious about a dog's tail, which is quite beyond our imagination to fathom. If you don't believe me grab your dog's ears and scrunch them around and shake his head from side to side or even kiss him on the lips without taking him to dinner first. He won't mind at all. In fact he will love you for it.

But if you grab - or even seem to be going to grab his tail he will frown and look worried. And you can see the frown only because he is able to face you with his back turned. Even if you had a tail, you couldn't do that, could you?

Imagine telling a joke at the office party, everyone standing with their backs turned to you so you'll know from their tails if they are laughing. And there could be no deception. If your joke weren't funny, nothing would wag. There would be no way they could get it to wag if it didn't want to.

Ok, here's an experiment for you. If you are owned by a rottwieler, who really loves you, why don't you grab his tail and give it a tug. He will be distressed. But dogs are very forgiving – eventually. I'll bet that when he comes to visit you in hospital he will wag his tail to say he's sorry.

He would have reacted more lovingly if you had kissed him on the lips instead of tugging his tail – unless you'd been eating garlic bread, then you would probably still be in hospital.

It's no accident that dogs became man's best friend and cats didn't. When a small dog climbs onto your lap it's because he loves you. A cat does it, because it's warmer there.

Now don't get me wrong; I've got nothing against cats. Sometimes I have a yearning to get really close to them – especially nights when they are wailing their love song outside my window – but they are usually too fast for me to show how much I care.

Cats, left to their own devises are thought to be more independent than dogs but it's simply not true. A cat, stalking a bird crouches and becomes almost catatonic – no pun intended – honestly. But watch its tail. The darn thing swishes from side to side; swish, swish, on and on. It can be seen from outer space. Look bird, here I am.

This is why cats always come home for dinner. Would they do that if they had been independently eating birds instead of needfully wailing outside my window?

But a dog stalks with his tail tucked between his legs and concentrates on not thinking of anything funny – like you saying that your dog will love you even if you don't give him bones. Well, there's a limit to how tightly you can clench your tail when you have no deception connection.

So, remember, if you need to make a speech, which includes a few jokes try it out on your dog first. If he frowns and his tail is rigid and trembling, quickly change your jokes. Oh, and if you have a rottweiler, wear a padded suit, or run like heck, OK?

3. BEWARE HEAVY DUTY STRING

We are constantly hearing arguments for and against gun control. Some say that the poor, much maligned 357 Magnum and its ilk are being unfairly targeted as death dealing devises and that people kill people, not guns.

It seems to me that this is probably true. Someone bent on mass murder and deprived of the poor innocent gun will soon find a more dangerous way to carry out his deadly purposes.

We would soon be reading of deranged, disgruntled ex-employees, dismissed for making rotten coffee, rushing into their ex-offices, wild eyed and wielding bits of string.

Newspapers will report that the killer rushed from desk to desk, strangling people at random. "He made us line up and wait our turn as he wound his bit of string around neck after neck," said a dazed woman. "The whole thing was over in 3 days," she cried. "There was nothing we could do. I was lucky because he ran out of string."

So it's quite obvious that mass murderers only use guns to carry out their desperate deeds because string is so difficult to come by. In fact I hear that the NRA is going to change its name to the NSA, (the national string association) a change, which will be reflected in its methods of hunting wild game.

Hunters will hide in the brush and when the quarry is two hundred yards away they will hurl their bit of string and strangle the beast. "Hey it's people who strangle game, not string," say's the NSA in answer to their critics who claim that string is cruel and should be outlawed.

It's quite obvious that if there were no guns, warring gangsters would carelessly mow down innocent bystanders with wild flurries of twine. Parents would be warned not to leave loaded string in the house where kids could find it. There would be string detectors at airports and schools. You see, unlike guns, string kills people – especially rapid firing string.

There is no doubt that the police will be very excited by the replacement of their guns with bits of string, which can really stop a perp dead. This is particularly true when it's placed around the neck at close quarters – especially when the officers are faced with criminals wielding harmless guns.

But desperate criminals are beginning to combat this new deadly string threat by using all kinds of unusual weapons in the commission of their nefarious deeds. One that is quite likely to become a favorite is a bag of prawn crackers. This is true and not something I conjured from the depths of my warped imagination.

Last week in London, England, 4 thieves robbed a Chinese food deliveryman by hitting him on the head with a lightweight bag of prawn crackers. Naturally this made him a little light headed. "I could have been killed," he wailed. "Why couldn't they have used a harmless gun like everybody else?" Well he didn't quite say that but he could have, couldn't he?

When Scotland Yard officers arrived on the scene they noticed a thin path of sauce, which had leaked from one of the containers. As we know, only legendary Scotland Yard detectives or Sherlock Holmes would have seen the significance of this. So the officer in charge followed the trail by walking on his knees and mopping up the sauce with his cheese sandwich.

9

Anyway, by time the officer had finished his lunch all the sauce was gone. But Scotland Yard officers have always been ruthless. They have always been contemptuous of harmless 357 Magnums and, instead carry dangerous bits of string to properly protect themselves from felons.

Well the trail led to an apartment where the police arrested three men and a woman. When threatened with heavy-duty string, the thieves dropped their bag of prawn crackers and surrendered. They were charged with possession of an offensive weapon with intent to consume two thousand calories.

The police remarked that people kill people, not prawn crackers – although, they found that prawn crackers are hard to resist, even if you threaten them with a loaded string.

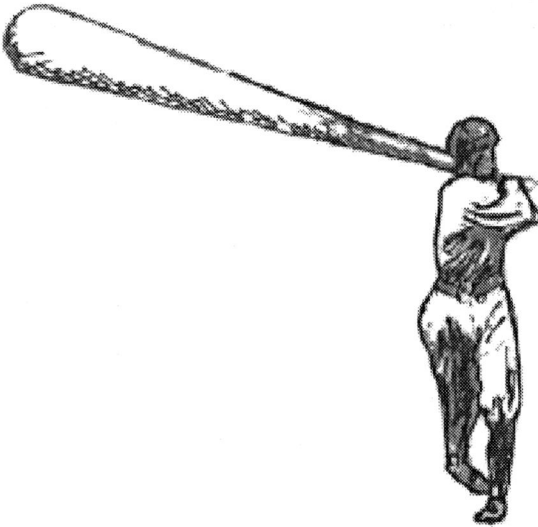

4. MAYBE THE BIG STICK COMES LATER

It's strange but there are very few sports that don't involve the use of a ball. Ice hockey and boxing are two that don't. But as the main objective of both games is to punch each other senseless, who needs a ball? A ball would just be in the way.

In Sumo wrestling the contestants themselves are the balls so you could probably call Sumo a game that's played with and by balls, both. If there are any Sumo wrestlers out there who object to this I would be glad to run and hide in the closet and jabber incoherent stuff like, "I'm sorry, I'm sorry, please don't sit on me."

Snooker is played with several balls and a stick. The game is judged not just by the color of the ball but by the contents of

11

its pockets. Basically, what you do is prod the ball with the stick over and over and see if you can make it angry.

If you keep prodding it into a pocket it will most likely make your opponent angry, depending on whether or not he thinks you're a hustler - in which case you would probably be better off with the Sumo wrestlers.

On the other hand Baseball is played with only one ball and a stick and it starts out being angry right off. It doesn't need any prodding. In fact in this game the ball is supposed to prod the stick instead of the other way around. It approaches at great speed with the object of missing the stick and hitting you. In the end you have to run for your life.

To save face, you can pretend you are just racing the ball to a base. The trick is to time your run so that nobody is quite sure who got there first. This usually makes people mad and they fight and spit and yell in each other's faces. Then they forget all about you and hurl the ball at someone else.

True, the vocabulary of the big league players is not as creative as that of the Little League parents. This is because the guys are concerned with being good role models and the parents just want their kid to win.

Pinball machines also rely on a sphere to score points. But the trouble with pinball is that it's harder to cheat. If you try to guide the ball by pushing and nudging the machine, it stops working and claims harassment.

Of course, as long as you don't actually move the machine, you are allowed to hunch your shoulders and sway from side to side and grunt. This will sometimes fool the machine into putting the ball where you want it.

But football, the most popular sport in America is played with an ellipse. However it's still a kind of ball. I guess it's shaped that way so that it's easier to carry in the hand. That's why it's called a football. If anyone can explain this to me I would be very surprised.

A soccer ball on the other hand is spherical for easy kicking with the foot. You are only allowed to touch it with your foot. That's why, in America, it's called a soccer ball and not a football. Are you still with me?

Marbles is played with tiny glass balls and a stick. Kids use thumb skills to determine who gets to take home all the marbles. The stick is usually brandished by a big guy with hairy knuckles. He usually gets to take home all the marbles. This rule applies even if he is not playing.

However, another rule of the game is never to tell this guy that he doesn't have all his marbles - unless, of course you enjoyed your encounter with the Sumo wrestlers.

Unlike marbles, golf is played with one ball and lots of sticks. You have to walk miles through woods and water and big holes filled with sand to find the ball - at least I do. It takes all day.

The one thing that places golf above the other games is that you don't get paid millions unless you win. Before you suggest that this rule be applied to Baseball just remember that baseball players carry big sticks.

13

You will notice that it's only the sports where there is a potential for violence between the players that are popular. You never hear of "shot putting" riots or wild "long jump" fans. Imagine how popular javelin throwing would be if it were played by a couple of angry teams.

Even the universe is played with balls. Whether a big stick will be involved at some later date is anybody's guess.

5. CONSULTANT

If you would like to become a multimillionaire, a giant of the New York Stock Exchange, own a yacht, a huge limo and a pair of Michael Jordan's sneakers; you've come to the right place. I can show you how to achieve the kind of success you are looking for and deserve.

No, I don't have any of these things myself. This is because I prefer the modest splendor of my 1956 Moped and the luxury of a bed-sit - if I can make up the rent arrears by Friday, that is.

Anyway, I'm here to help you achieve your goals. You are probably not very rich at the moment or you would be in Acapulco instead of seeking the services of a consultant. Well, my experience has taught me that before you can get rich, the first thing you will need is some money.

This will mean approaching your bank manager in a confidant manner. You must learn to curl your lip and sneer at him. Or put your feet up on his desk - whichever seems right at the moment.

He will immediately warm to you, and ask if there is anything he can do to help. This is the catch. This could be your stumbling block if you don't get it right. The only way he is going to lend you money is if you can prove you don't need it.

Are you with me so far? If you can figure out how to do this, I hope you will let me know so that I can pay my rent by Friday.

I had a letter from a young man of 18 who has already developed some excellent methods of accumulating other people's money without actually using a firearm.

He says he is trying to get his life together financially, which is quite commendable, considering the short time he has had to tear it apart. "I am trying to pay off my enormous credit card debt so that I will have some money available to invest," he says.

If it were not for a collection on his credit report, he says he would transfer his balances from high interest to low interest cards - then he could borrow more on the first cards which would be all paid up, or something like that.

Well, because of my vast experience in financial matters, it's clear to me that this lad is the stuff that millionaires are made of - or the stuff of which millionaires are made - depending on how insufferably pedantic you are and if you are interested in becoming rich or an English professor.

Anyway, I told the plausible lad to visit my bank manager who deserves this kind of borrower after the way he treated me.

Bank managers can be very picky, you see. They ask lots of irrelevant questions before giving you money, like, have you ever had a paying job? That's so ridiculous. If you had a paying job why would you need his money? But I advised the young man not to use that response - although it would be interesting to see if the manager calls security again.

My advice to would-be-millionaires is to do as I'm doing; become a consultant. But always be sure to take your fee before the client takes your advice. To be successful in this business you must never leave yourself open to the insinuation that you're advice was completely wrong.

This rule applies especially when the aspersion is cast by a breathless voice on the phone from the bankruptcy court. Your advice at this point is "keep calm," and "every cloud has a silver lining" and other stuff like that. This is always greatly appreciated by someone who is in the depths of despair and contemplating suicide.

Here is one example of the kind of advice you can offer a new client. It's open to misinterpretation and could give you an out. It goes something like this, and can vary according to whether the client becomes violent or not. Investing/speculating in bonds is as potentially risky as investing/speculating in stocks." At this point your client could become quite excited.

So you go on. "That is, when interest rates rise, bond prices fall. Thus, you will probably see lower prices for your shares of the bond fund." Here you might give your ambiguous suggestions a final defensive flourish with the words, "What you should do now depends on whether you are truly an investor - or a speculator."

If the client is in your office at the time, you smile knowingly. If you are communicating by mail, don't sign the letter and wipe off all fingerprints.

Strangely enough, people have become rich on worse advice than this.

But now I'm going to call my own consultant. He says he has a master plan, which will enable me to pay my rent arrears by Friday - or, at least his own, if he can get me to pay my fee up front.

6. DOGS LOVE BONES UNCONDITIONALLY

The most wonderful thing about dogs is that they love us unconditionally. When we come home late and look into those trusting eyes, do they ever say to us, "Now where have you been till this time of night, buster?" Of course not. They don't care where we've been as long as it includes the store that sells dog food.

And dogs are not just loving, they are smart and discriminating. This is why they know how lovable we are. Cats are not so unconditional they will sometimes sit on your lap and give you a disdainful look that says, "I'm only sitting here because it's warmer than the windowsill."

Anyway, you may have heard that we have a large standard poodle called Fifi. Of course I know she is not the smartest or best dog in the world because you have that dog yourself. It's quite true that many of your friends and neighbors believe that their dog is the one, but you know there can only be one best dog and it's yours unless you have more than one, then all your dogs are the best dog.

You probably have the same problem with those greeting cards that say "To the best mother in the world." Isn't it silly that they print so many cards every year just for your Mom when no one else is going to need them anyway?

But it should be said that Fifi doesn't love everyone unconditionally. If she hears a strange man at the door she won't love him at all and will tell him so. She is, after all, a dangerous watchdog, and if the strange man should break into the house she will only love him on condition that he doesn't frown at her; then she will whimper. But, if he brings a bone every day she will unlock the door while he's coming up the street. Only a dog can love like that.

The main reason we love our dogs so much is because they are dumb. If they could speak there would come a time when they would express an opinion that sounded sexist or racist or, well, opinionated. That would start the rot.

But dogs are smarter than that. They are certainly not dumb enough to let us know they can speak. This is because they are well aware that being dumb is a dog's greatest asset. They know very well that even if they were able to recite the soliloquy from Hamlet, they would be well advised to do it alone, at night and for their own amusement - as cats do.

An absolutely true example from many years ago is the case of Bonzo. On our way to school, we kids would often see a black faced chimney sweep cycling through the streets on his appointed rounds. He wore a grimy top hat and sloping over his shoulder, like a rifle, were the rods that held his circular flu brushes.

Occasionally, as he cycled, puffs of soot streamed out behind him like stardust. But, to us kids, his magical and aristocratic bearing was overshadowed by Bonzo, a sooty little black and white Bull Terrier that followed his master through the dismal streets of London as fast as his little legs could carry him.

When the sweep entered a house, Bonzo would remain outside, nose pointing skyward, and bark when the sweep's brush appeared through the top of the chimney. Thus poor Bonzo earned his keep, rain or shine, day after day. Oh, Bonzo, Bonzo, Bonzo; and we thought you were so smart because you could talk. You would have been so much better off to have kept your trap shut, wouldn't you?

What's the point of being cute and having a waggly tail, if you don't bother to enslave someone who will grant your every wish? And why would a smart dog want to go out to work and come home and cook the dinner and feed the dog when she can simply gaze into someone's eyes, and by cocking her head on one side have anything in the world she wants?

I mean, come on be honest, what would you do if you had a waggly tail and could cock your head on one side?

I don't like to keep coming back to Fifi but she has so many qualities that should be acknowledged. For one thing, she will eat or destroy anything we leave on the coffee table. Sometimes she will tear up a napkin or eat the TV guide.

Now you may not think that's very lovable but, you see, she never touches the remote control. She wreaks havoc on everything else but leaves the remote strictly alone. Can any dog have greater unconditional love than that? Of course she likes to watch the news on TV but, just the same, I like to think it's unconditional.

Still it's amazing the awful things we've done in the name of love to change the proud wolf into poodles and dachshunds. Fifi's fur is cut to look as if she is wearing a white fluffy sweater and panty hose. And she has a white fur ball at the end of her shaved tail, like a hirsute lollipop that she can never quite reach. I can't imagine what Jack London would have made of her. I don't think he would have called her "Fang."

So, although we know Fifi loves us unconditionally, we keep a spare remote on a high shelf in case she happens to look in the mirror one day and sees her haircut. No love could be that unconditional.

7. *ABOUT MISTAKES I MAY NOT HAVE MADE*

This column was first published October 22nd 2000 in the Hanford Sentinel, almost two weeks before George Bush was elected President for the first time. Nothing has been changed from the original.

"Now listen up, Georgie, I'm your dad, and I've been president and you haven't. And if you want to lead the free world and have people respect your judgment and be in charge of the doomsday button, you better do what your ol dad says, okay?"

George W. pouts

"But, Dad, I'm a big boy now, and yesterday I made a decision all on my own"

"Oh, George, George, George, what color socks you wear with your swim shorts is not so much a presidential decision as sartorial preference."

George W. sneers crookedly and decides it's time his dad learned that his boy can't be fooled by big words.

"Well, maybe, Dad, but I still think socks is about the way I dress not my choice of a vacation spot in the Greek Islands."

"George, just shut your mouth, for a minute, will you?"

George W. pouts again.

"Hey, Dad, you won't be able to speak to me like that when I'm president, you know. You'll have to say shut your mouth Mr. President. I'm not a kid you know."

"Oh, I don't mind that, son, just as long as your mouth gets shut when I say.

George W. glares at his dad then stands up and walks manfully towards a picture of Lincoln and sticks his gum on the frame for later use - not the frame, the gum. His dad had warned him about his lack of frugality. "Giving up my gum will learn him I can deny myself when I want," he thinks.

"Listen, Georgie. One thing I learned as president is that you have got to be very careful whom you choose as running mate."

"What do you mean, Dad? You said I done well with Dick Cheney."

"Well, it looks that way but there's just one thing you need to do to be sure."

"Ooh, ooh, I know dad, offer him shares in Saudi Oil."

George senior begins to cry softly. Then he gets up, un-sticks the gum from Lincoln's picture and begins to chew sadly.

"But son, you don't own Saudi Oil."

"No, no, Dad, I mean after I become president."

George Senior decides to ignore this in case he is questioned about it later when the congress is in uproar and all out war with the Middle East imminent.

"What I mean son is you have to make sure that your running mate can spell "tomato". Look what happened to me: I lost the election."

"Well, Dad, you can't be expected to know everything just because you're president. tomato is a hard word to spell, I know I couldn't..."

"Not me, you dolt; Dan Quayle. If it hadn't been for him I would have beaten Bill Clinton."

"Yeah, right, Dad."

"Anyway, I keep getting sidetracked. Now I know how those journalists feel. What I'm saying is, Al Gore is trying to fool all of the people all of the time. Only Bill can do that. So you just gotta try to fool most of the people until after the election, the way it's usually done.

"You mean I have to choose sides, Dad?"

"That's right son, you have to be honest and straightforward. Let people know what you stand for. Go after something solid and respectable - like the anti-Semitic vote."

George W. looks horrified, not just because his father stole his gum but because of his suggestion that he should appeal to liberals.

"Dad, that is so clinical of you.

"Don't you mean cynical, Georgie?"

"Sure, Dad, if you like it better, why not?"

"What I'm saying is, don't be a Jerry Springer, throwing mud and showing people the ugly side of America; you can't win like that.

You mean no telling the truth about Al Gore?

That's right. So what's your new plan Georgie?"

"What I'm thinking, Dad, is to tell people to read my lips, then if things don't work out the way they think, I tell them they read wrong and they should brush up on their reading condescension."

"Don't you mean reading comprehension, son?"

"I wish you would stop asking me what I mean. I'm having enough trouble with that as it is. Anyway Dad, I was honest with the public. I told them that I've learned from mistakes I may or may not have made."

"Oh, and what did you learn from the mistakes you may not have made, son?"

"George W. watches his dad who is now chewing much more vigorously on the nicotine gum he stole from Lincoln's frame.

"Why are you being mean to me, Dad? After all, I am the son of a president. That should help me win, shouldn't it"?

"Well, I gotta tell you, son, in this country people don't take too kindly to nepotism."

"Well, I don't believe in nepotism either, Dad, I just think people should give the juiciest jobs to their relatives, don't you?"

"Son, I can see you are going to make a great leader of the free world, and it makes me very proud. All I can say is God help... I mean God bless America. Now go off and play with your new oil well, I've got a call to make."

"Oh, hello Mrs. Springer, is Jerry home? Okay, just tell him I said if he can spell tomato he has a great future behind him – I mean, ahead of him."

"No, I'm not being clinical Mrs. Springer. it's just that I've had a funny day and I'm having a little trouble with my reading condescension.

8. MAYBE I WAS MISINFORMED, DAD

This column was first published February 30th 2003 in the Hanford Sentinel three weeks before the start of the war in Iraq. Nothing has been changed from the original column.

"Oh, hi, Dad, can you hear me? It's George W. I'm in a foreign country, can you hear me?"

"Well, just about, son – er - Mr. President. We don't get very good reception living in cave shelters up in the Yukon.

"Listen, dad, you'll be so proud. I've just taken over this Ayrab country called Eyeraq."

"That's good, Congress is getting tired of living in the Yukon and your mom's frowning a lot because of Dick Cheney's startling cave drawings."

"But they kept you safe from all those nuclear bombs and invading armies of 2 million troops."

"Cheney's drawings?"

"No, Dad, the cave shelters."

"Listen up Georgie, Iraq doesn't have nuclear bombs or 2 million troops or aircraft carriers or submarines?

"Are you sure, Dad? Have I been misinformed like when someone told Humphrey Bogart to go to Casablanca for the waters?"

"Listen son, the country that's got nuclear bombs and missiles and 2 million troops is North Korea."

"Oh, gosh darn it, you mean I should have turned right at Japan? But it's okay, Dad. We'll have the oil fires out in twenty years, and then I'll go and get Korea for you. Any idea what country mom would like?

"No, Mr. president, but I guess this means we've got to stay in the Yukon for another twenty years - but wait a minute, son. Ooh, ooh, I know, send the French to North Korea. They only want to fight someone who's a real danger to the world. Tell them Korea's canceling 4-hour lunch breaks.

"Okay, Dad, but, apart from Dick Cheney, you're doing okay, right?"

"Well we're gonna have a problem with the bears and mountain lions when we run out of Democrats to throw them."

"You should have stocked up on Germans and Russians, when you had the chance, like I told you. Dad."

"Yeah, and Clintons got the bears convinced that he's going to catch the guy that stole their porridge, and they know he wouldn't lie to them."

"But what about Gore, Dad?"

"Well, Georgie, he said he wasn't going to run any more, but you should have seen him go when he was being chased by that big grizzly"

"Anyway, Dad, like I said, I've got this country, see."

"Oh right, son, so what are you going to do with it?"

"Well, that's why I called. What did you do with Japan when you took it over?"

"Son, you're not going to like this but I gave it back."

"Oh, yeah, Dad, they didn't have much oil, did they?

"Just whale oil, son.

"What I think Dad, is I'll make it into a state."

"You can't do that, son it belongs to the Arabs."

"Don't say that, Dad; you're making me stamp my foot in rage."

You still do that? I thought you stopped that when you were 32. Okay, make it into a state but you make your brother governor, you hear? It'll be easier than Florida. This time he'll have tanks to help him get the votes for you.

"Anyway, Dad, what I called about is, Saddam has detonated the oil wells, which are now engulfed in a devastating conflagration exposing the entire middle east to a suffocating, noxious pall of deadly, black smoke."

"Someone wrote that down for you, son, didn't they?"

"Gosh darn it, Dad, how did you know? Saddam said he wouldn't tell anyone."

"Anyway, son, you did promise to make life better for them. And, I'm sure they would rather have suffocation than food rationing."

"Listen, You gotta help me, Dad. I wanna come home. Can you get me out of this owning Iraq problem?

"Well, son. I guess you really are between Iraq and a hard place. So what you do is this. You hang on until the election, and let the Democrats win. Of course, that means we can't let the bears eat Clinton. He's about our only chance of losing. And he'll probably convince the Iraqis that they're better off, too.

9. BEWARE THE GIRL NEXT DOOR

Do you like your job? Is it more than just a way to earn a living? Is it an integral factor in defining who you are and a necessary dynamic by which you measure your worth to society? Would you continue to do it if you won 85 million dollars on the lottery? Okay, okay, just kidding. I wanted to see if you were awake.

So, discounting a lottery win, all we can do to be happy is to find a job where we are appreciated. But if you are unhappy in your job, you should, at least test the water carefully before deciding to leave for greener pastures. Yes, I'm mixing metaphors but I'm not looking for a job, am I?

Anyway, look for signs that your job offers a chance of advancement. But if your boss tells you he is grooming you for a better position, be careful.

A better position could mean anything. I mean his idea of a better position might be to change yours from sitting in a chair to kneeling on the floor with your monitor on the ceiling. Don't fall for that one. I know I'll never fall for it again.

Or maybe he'll say your new position is good for the company because he can then give your desk to the guy who will soon be in your previous position in your chair. This may sound exciting, but look out for a down side. Of course being on your knees all day does make it more convenient to ask forgiveness from a wrathful deity who is obviously well and truly irritated with one or two of your trespasses.

It's true that you should only stay with a company where you feel you can make a difference - and yes, you are making a difference if the company used to make a profit before you joined, and now it doesn't. But you shouldn't boast about this to your boss. If he were unaware of your talent in this respect you wouldn't be on your knees.

Perhaps you have decided to accept the new kneeling position. That's fine, but it does make me wonder what persuaded you to leave your last job. I mean I can't help wondering just how bad it was; and I'm really, really, afraid to ask in case the horror of it keeps me awake at night.

However, if you are turned down for the kneeling position and are forced to remain seated in a cubicle, you should try to improve your standing in the company by spending more time sitting in the office. So how is your standing improved by sitting? Don't ask me, I'm as confused as you are. I guess it's just a mystery - like why are Michael Jackson's brothers black.

But spending all your time at the office does not necessarily mean your social life will be compromised. What you must do is transfer your social life to the office. You must have heard of guys marrying the girl next door.

So check out the next cubicle. Invite the occupant on a date to the water cooler or stroll hand in hand together through your boss's office. They say that all the world loves a lover. Your boss will soon let you know if this little saying is true.

You might even risk a kiss on the cheek at the copier. You should not do any of this when the occupant of the next cubicle is not a girl but a large, hairy guy with a black belt in kickboxing. He may get the wrong idea. So, no kiss on the cheek on your first stroll, okay?

Still, it might be worth the inconvenience if he is the boss's nephew. It depends on how ambitious you are.

Now I don't wish to rain on your parade, (whatever that means) but if you follow my advice and still fail, your only hope is to keep buying lottery tickets. You can be sure that if you do win 85 million dollars, the hairy guy in the next cubicle will develop a sudden urge to walk you to the water cooler and kiss your cheek. Perhaps you should take up kick boxing, just in case.

10. DANCING AROUND THE TRUTH

It's not easy to know when someone is lying to you. Even the rack and thumbscrews are not infallible. But don't give up. Giant intellects are now laboring hard to unravel the secrets of this skill, which if universally mastered could increase the divorce rate by at least 150%.

So far they have discovered that people act out of character when they lie. You have to possess a giant intellect to notice this.

Okay, to illustrate: If you have just persuaded a used car salesman to sell you a rusty old 1958 Ford Edsel for 20,000 dollars and he says, "Not now, madam, I have to go and send flowers to my mother," is he acting out of character?

Since I don't possess a giant intellect, I don't know. I mean, is he lying about the flowers and his mother to get out of the sale? If so, I think it shows there is more to him than just being a liar. He is obviously an idiot as well.

Perhaps he was just confused. He should have lied about the car first and then sent flowers to his mother after you believed him about the car. This is because he wasn't acting out of character when he lied about the car, so he would appear to be telling the truth. He only appeared to lie when he told the truth about his mother. Are you still with me?

Okay, I guess we can all understand why the experts didn't go into this. I'm beginning to wonder why I did.

Of course some people are better at lying than others. Take politicians, for example. I would say the only president who ever got into power without lying was George Washington. And this was because there was no one running against him. Oh, maybe he lied to his wife when he promised not to do anything dangerous, but he meant standing under falling cherry trees, not standing in a boat crossing the Potomac, so that doesn't count.

Then someone said, "I did not give my socks to that woman." I mean how do you judge someone who is only in character when he's lying? And what do you look for when he's telling the truth but deliberately making it sound like a lie?

Why would he want to make it sound like a lie, you ask. Okay, question: "Have you been giving your socks to that woman Bill?"

Answer: "Oh, yeah, right, I was giving her my socks right there in the oval office while everybody was right outside the door sniggering." Would he be acting out of character or in it? Perhaps he had discovered that if you tell the truth and smile, nobody will believe you. That's something else the experts left alone.

According to these experts someone is probably lying if there is a sudden change in the pitch of their voice. This means rappers never lie - Although it would be nice if they would change their pitch sometimes. Geographically would do just fine.

Evidently it's a danger sign when someone suddenly turns his body away from you. Of course, if he were watering the lawn or something, the opposite would be true.

Another thing to watch for is nervous movement of the feet and legs, which casts doubt on whether Gene Kelly was really dancing in the rain, as he claimed, or using special effects.

It seems to me that to establish the truth you should first ask a few innocuous questions. You might want a truthful opinion from a girl you are sweet on at the office. Innocuous question: "Do you think Brad Pitt is handsome?" If she says yes, you may notice that she is smiling dreamily and her eyes are warm.

Then pop the real question: "Do you think I'm handsome?" Sometimes this can be tricky. I mean if she says yes, then starts to shuffle her feet and turns her body away from you or throws up on your shoes, is she really lying or was she lying about Brad Pitt.

The answer sometimes depends on your own level of self-deception as much as the truthfulness of the person you are questioning. Basically if your own feet start to shuffle it means you are lying to yourself. Okay, so did George Bush the elder, only say, "read my lips," so we wouldn't watch his feet? The experts are still out on that one.

11. STAR CROSSED LOVERS

We happy romantics of the free world have just participated in the rituals of yet another St. Valentine's day. We've had the love and the kisses, the hearts and flowers and chocolates and stuff and now it's time for the reality check. So, let's be honest. Love can be a terrible nuisance, sometimes. And the most irritating thing about love is that, unlike deep do-do, you can never be quite sure when you are in it. Not really.

Okay, yes, you know when you fall out of it, which means that you must have been in it before, but then it's too late, isn't it? So when this happens just tell her you're sorry. She'll understand, I promise.

What you say is: "look, when I gave you that Valentine's card pledging my love 'until the end of time,' it should have said, 'until 3 o'clock Saturday afternoon.'" This is the bit where you kneel and say, "And can I have the chocolates back?" She may get a little violent if you follow this with, 'it's not you it's me.'" After all, that's what Valentine's Day is all about: Chocolates, right?

Oh, and If you gave her a diamond necklace, forget it. That's a keeper. You'll have to buy yourself another one – maybe real diamonds this time.

You probably think I'm a cynic, but that's what they call people who say things that are unpleasant but true. No one minds if you say things that are pleasant and untrue - and who cares as long as you get your chocolates back.

Throughout history there has been a surfeit of stories about lovers and I defy you to name one that had a happy ending. Shakespeare called his lovers, "star crossed," I don't know what that means but I would guess that no one got their chocolates back.

You must have heard of Abelard and Heloise. Well, come on, it was only 900 years ago – how soon we forget. Anyway, Heloise was the daughter of a French cleric and Abelard was her teacher.

So one day, they were discovered by Heloise's uncle. Well, he didn't discover them, you know, not like Columbus with America. I mean he knew they were there all along. He just discovered what they were doing.

They were both sent to live in separate monasteries forever. I know you'll say I'm being cynical again but I'll bet the monastery that put in the highest bid got Heloise.

And what about Aphrodite? According to Homer, she was married to hephaestus, the lame and ugly god of fire. Then she ran off with Ares the God of war. Well there was no way hephaestus was going to demand his chocolates back while Ares was around, was there? Not if he valued his good leg, that is.

In a Midsummer Night's Dream, under Pucks spell, Titania falls in love with Bottom, the weaver. Hence Titania's lament: "Oh, my Bottom, I love you from the bottom of my heart but, tell me, am I loved by the heart of my Bottom?" Now, I ask you, how would that look on a Valentine's card? And, anyway, she had been in love with Oberon until 3 o'clock Saturday.

The only sensible part of the story is that Puck has turned Bottom into a monster with an Asses head. Well, what woman hasn't fallen for someone like that?

At the end of Antony and Cleopatra, Antony falls on his sword. And no, he wasn't accident-prone. He actually did it because he thought Cleopatra had done it first. Anyway, he was wrong about Cleopatra and when she found out how stupid – I mean romantic - he was she let an asp bite her on her... Well, on her way out of town to shuffle off this mortal coil.

Virtually the same fate befell those star-crossed-lovers, Romeo and Juliet. In their case, Romeo thought Juliet was dead so he poisoned himself. Then she woke up and saw he was dead and kissed him and poisoned herself on his lips – and you thought herpes was a problem.

Anyway, this whole love thing seems more suited to Halloween than St. Valentine's Day. - and the irony is that although not everyone got to keep the chocolates, everyone still managed to come to a sticky end, didn't they?

But, sometimes I do wonder why I never get any valentine's cards. Oh, well, maybe it was something I said.

12. LOOKING FOR LOVE
IN ALL THE WRONG PLACES

Not too long ago, if you had said you were looking for love on the web, amorous flies would have flocked to your parlor. But, today, lonely hearts really are looking for someone to cling to on the Internet Web – which is aptly named, since it serves much the same purpose as the original. And you can even get advice on how to weave it.

Internet dating coach, Debra Livingston, of New York, met her own boyfriend online. Her advice is: "Ask friends and family for advice." Well that's a good start. I mean, if that'll do it, why do you need her?

Anyway, it seems like an easy job to me. So I'm going to help you out. Well, first of all, if you can't get a date among the teeming millions of New York, but get one on the Web, It's clear that you are mostly popular with people who have never actually met you.

This is okay, because when you meet someone on the Web, you will have found a kindred spirit. You have both been limited by looking for love in all the wrong places like, well, like among the teeming millions of New York.

Naturally, you must be careful never to actually meet your Web date. I mean, if you plan to do that, you might just as well go back to the singles' bar, right?

And why on earth would you want to go to a singles bar where you'll only meet people who had to go to a singles bar to meet... Okay, you'll still be with kindred spirits, all yearning for love, or something - and all pretending they came in by mistake.

"Oh, hello, what are you doing here?"

"Hi, I'm waiting for a bus, how about you?"

Well, for crying out loud, everyone knows what you're doing here, don't they. It's a singles bar, for heaven's sake.

At least, on the Web it's like you met by accident and fell in love by clicking the wrong button - and, of course you don't have to look at each other.

Sure, you may fall in love with Yassir Arafat, but you'll never know, will you? So, if you do plan to meet, make it somewhere dark where you can pretend he's Cary Grant – somewhere really dark – like a coalmine.

On the net, everyone is looking for Cary Grant or Deborah Kerr (you don't really know if this shows my age or not. Maybe I just like to date older people, okay?)

Debra Livingston says, "be honest, but be careful when meeting people you've talked to online." So, what have I just been saying? Don't meet them, okay? Spend your lives together separately, online. Let your mouse or mouses or mice or whatever, grow old together.

Of course as an advisor, I should also help those of you who have a desperate, primal need to actually meet your online date.

Well, okay, you've been communicating by keyboard, but real conversation is different. To be successful, you must learn the art and seductive magic of verbal thrust and parry. You do not say stuff like, "you sounded thinner on the Web."

Sometimes you men might find a woman who is even shyer than you are. She may have trouble making conversation. She may not talk at all. This alone could cause some men to propose on the first date.

However, you men should be aware that this advice deals mainly with the subject of meeting and relating to women from a shy man's perspective. So if you are a lothario or a Casanova or a gigolo this is not for you. And where would you find the time, anyway? Also, being a foreigner, you wouldn't understand the written instructions.

When Livingston says, "be honest." she is basically right. Then she says, "Make your first sentence a grabber." Okay, but, take my advice, go slowly. If your wife ran away and left you with five kids under the age of seven, try not to blurt it out as soon as you meet. You will find you are grabbing all the wrong places. Yes, it will save you the price of dinner but it won't get you a baby sitter for your five kids.

Having said all that I suspect that nature might soon give evolution an unexpected boost to facilitate the survival of the human race. Someday people will meet only in chat rooms and fall in love by clicking on to each other. And they will produce offspring by increasing the capacity of their hard drive

Some lucky stiffs will be born with a mouse at the end of their arm instead of a hand so they can double click in private whenever the mood takes them.

As for me, I think I'd rather meet Deborah Kerr at the top of the Empire State Building. Okay, maybe I'd accept Meg Ryan if Deborah has an accident.

13. OUT IN LEFT FIELD

Everyone knows that playing ball games builds character. This is especially true of baseball. It has the power to transform poor, irresponsible boys into rich, irresponsible men. Nothing else in the world can be as inspiring as the sight of embryo baseball stars learning to chew. But it must be said that Mrs. Winterbottom, my history teacher, could have taught them a thing or two about hitting a spittoon at ten paces.

The power of baseball to impart mathematical skills is demonstrated in the words of the great Yogi Berra who, among other things, said "You give a hundred percent in the first half of the game, and if it isn't enough, in the second half you give what's left."

This is not something that's easy to do. Today's baseball stars, sentimental traditionalists that they are, apply the same method of calculating when negotiating their salaries.

But who among us can resist the magic of the boys of summer? The sweet sound of leather on aluminum. Still, it should be remembered that there is a lot more to baseball than the glamour and the glory. There is also a well established etiquette to be followed. Anyone can scratch but a successful player must learn to scratch with nonchalance and detachment as if someone else is doing it and it's not his fault.

Baseball takes dedication and application. There are all kinds of skills to be learned; but something every player should remember when carrying out maneuvers such as spitting, scratching, and adjusting sports equipment, is that timing is everything. This is because if all the players do it at exactly the same time it could make some people nostalgic for the lovely chorus line at radio City; then it's every man for himself.

Well, now that you've learned about all the hard stuff you shouldn't have any trouble with the game itself. It involves simple things like learning to pitch and slide and score home runs.

One of the great benefits of the game is that all the real stars learn to converse in a series of mysterious hand signals - as some of us do when we are cut off on the freeway.

In England it's not baseball but cricket that transforms belligerent young skinheads into belligerent old skinheads. Almost every English schoolboy must learn to play cricket. This is because they are taught from infancy that it's the very epitome of fair play and sportsmanship. It is their first introduction to the democratic ideal of freedom of choice.

It would have done your heart good to see the enthusiasm with which the boys at my old school fought their way into the locker room, trying to be first in to bat when given the alternative of hand to hand combat with the girl's hockey team.

Still, if not for our kindly coach we would never have heard the gentle derisive laughter of those wonderful nurses in the emergency room as they pried cricket balls from our mouths and put our teeth in little packets as keepsakes.

That it did, in fact, help to engender our spirit of sportsmanship as evidenced by the sporting behavior of drunken British soccer fans at international games.

Contrary to popular opinion cricket is not boring. In fact, nobody who has played cricket, summer after wonderful summer, year after year, could ever be bored again. Those hours of waiting in the sun saying "Well played old boy" and "It's time for tea and crumpets my good fellow," will invariably provide lifelong immunity to all kinds of boredom. Although baseball, being a close cousin, is almost as affective.

You have to actually play cricket to really appreciate the sheer joy of the game. A cricket ball is as heavy and hard as a baseball and travels at least as fast. I'll never forget the magic of my first game. Well, it's the purpose of the pitcher (bowler) to strike the wicket with the ball. Ha! I thought smugly; there's no way he can hit the wicket with my leg in front of it.

Well, I'm glad to say I no longer walk with a limp. You see, I had mistakenly understood the umpire's cry of "leg before wicket!" to be a suggestion that I use it as a winning ploy rather than a warning that I would be called "out" and have my leg broken if it were in front of the wicket. This will also explain why I prefer to play marbles.

In case you're wondering, cricket, which is baseballs first cousin was born in England in 1352. In the hallowed halls of oxford, learned men with puckered brows were trying to decide whether to invent cricket or Windows 95. Well we all know what big a mistake they made. But when the decision was finally reached, the waiting throng out in the square rattled their sabers indicating that the peasants weore revolting. "Give us Widows 95" they yelled "not bats and balls." "This is not cricket" they cried but, of course, as we now know, that's exactly what it was.

Anyway, today, in the hallowed halls of Oxford there is another meeting of great minds discussing the benefits of introducing some new rules to cricket like chewing and spitting and scratching while adjusting pieces of sporting equipment. And my personal favorite; the umpire and the coach in an eye popping, spit swapping, nose to nose screaming exhibition of true sportsmanship. Well, it's got to be safer than fighting the girl's hockey team.

14. WHAT DID YOU SAY

We are told that, these days, some High School graduates need help when filling out their university application forms. This is because they have a little trouble reading the questions.

But the problem is that, even after they master their letters, the university of their choice will still insist they understand the meaning of what they are reading.

Well, reading comprehension is a difficult concept for anyone to grasp. This is because you will need to be really good at it before you can comprehend a book that tells you how to do it. If you are already confused don't worry, we all need a little help now and then. So I'll give you a few hints.

It's important to see through the rhetoric. Take Don Quixote, for instance. He wasn't really a refugee from the Jerry Springer show. He was in fact just an ordinary, everyday guy who wore a brass barber's basin on his head and danced with windmills. Well, who doesn't know someone like that?

Sometimes even Charles Dickens can be baffling. I mean, why is the tale of a miser running around in his nightshirt and making whimpering sounds called "A Christmas Carol." Nobody sings a note. Oh, some of them rattle their chains and moan but that's not the same.

Well, what the story actually means is that if you scare someone enough they will give you a turkey at Christmas. Simplify, simplify. Some teachers have different interpretations so just choose the one you like best.

But I should warn you that some books are more difficult to understand than others. For a start, "Anna Karenina," and "Crime and Punishment" are tough. Even the Russians - who read Russian - are still trying to figure out what the authors were trying to say; but of course, now that we want to question them they are all conveniently dead. So you're out of luck.

Hemingway is a must to test you're talents. In "A Moveable Feast" he very skillfully weaves a colorful tapestry of the wild young years of a lost generation in Paris. It's savagely written, full of love and hope. The pages are redolent with the seductive aroma of coffee and the pungent fumes of absinthe and scotch. See what I mean about rhetoric?

Now, I'm going to help you out by telling you what the book is really all about. It's about Ernest. What he thinks, how he feels, what he does, and who he does it to.

While his wife and infant son are living, virtually penniless, over a sawmill in Paris, he is out gambling, skiing, eating oysters, drinking dry white wine and having chats with a plethora of now famous writers.

No, I don't know how many there are in a plethora. Or if it's more or less than a myriad. If you find out please let me know.

Well kids, I know that you are all sitting on the edge of your seats with excitement, waiting to learn more about Anna Karenina. So I'll give you a clue. The secret to understanding books by Tolstoy is to be found in his first few lines.

But look out for exceptions to this rule: In "Anna Karenina" he starts out by saying: "Happy families are all alike; every unhappy family is unhappy in its own way." It goes on:

"Everything was confusion in the Oblonskys' house." Well, I'm not surprised; I'm confused myself. So, in this case you will need to read the whole book. Sorry. Still, it's a lot easier than comprehending Hemingway, isn't it?

I don't think we need to go into the meaning of "The Catcher in the Rye" or "The Pitcher of Dorian Grey" because you probably know enough about baseball already.

Anyway, some schools are starting to teach reading comprehension before the students can actually read. This is so that they will be ready for it when the time comes - say when they're around thirty five or so.

Naturally, being unable to read makes studying at university a little more difficult. So illiterate students will be asked to explain the meaning of something a little easier than Dostoyevsky. It's all very well to say: Once upon "a time" the prince kissed sleeping beauty. But at what time was it once upon? Her parents will want to know. Was it 9, 9.30, 10, or what? That kind of thing.

Of course, for a well-rounded education there are other important areas of study. Someone once said: "If we don't study history we will be doomed to repeat it."

Unfortunately, they meant only the bad bits so it's no good refusing to read about the good bits hoping you'll get to do them again.

But, I don't want you to dismiss history as being an old fashioned thing of the past; it's not. Well, it is a thing of the past but... Anyway, you see what I mean about reading comprehension.

However, if you still find all this stuff too much trouble for you, why don't you just read Don Quixote - and let me know how it ends. I've often wondered.

15. WISH UPON A STAR SIGN

There are not too many people who know how to correctly interpret and manipulate the host of helpful hints handed out by their daily newspaper astrologer.

One trick is to be selectively skeptical. This means you only believe in astrology when the stars say what you want to hear. I mean, if you have tickets for the big game and your stars say it would be a good day to clean the garage, you laugh nonchalantly and say, "What a load of rubbish."

Of course, if your sign is "Gemini" you give the paper to your twin and say, "Hey, it's for you," then walk away. This will satisfy the stars. You can placate your twin later by giving a commentary on the game he missed. Just try to be imaginative and manipulative. It will bring out the best in you and make you popular.

Naturally, you will not be skeptical when your stars say, "Your personality draws others to you and you are even more lovable than usual." This is because, today, your horoscope confirms everything you already knew. So you leave it on the table for your spouse to see, and listen for the usual corroborating cries of "how true, how true."

Also, it's important to check the stars every day in case your spouse's horoscope says, "Today is a good day to clean the garage." You don't want to miss this when it happens because the garage must be in a terrible mess if you keep going to the game every time your horoscope is wrong.

But seeking guidance from the stars has been going on a long time. The Chinese practiced astrology 4000 years ago This was very necessary because when everyone is equal how do you decide who should clean the garage unless the stars tell you?

However, the Chinese Emperor's horoscope never ever hinted that he should clean the garage. Mostly he was advised by his stars to separate himself from things that offend his delicate nature. On those days he simply stopped watching PBS during pledge break. Sorry, but you have to be an Emperor to do that.

Of course If the Emperor's horoscope had advised him to give all the peasants fortune cookies, he would have sneered and said "What a load of rubbish this astrology is," and beheaded the astrologer. There is no need to be this drastic unless you really hate cleaning the garage.

However, being skeptical or misinterpreting your horoscope can be a bit tricky. Socrates was pretty smart yet when his stars said, "this is a good day to drink herbal tea" he left his coke in the Fridge and had a cup of hemlock instead. Well, you've just got to misinterpret the message correctly. But, looking on the bright side he didn't have to worry about the garage anymore.

2500 years ago, Pythagoras and Plato had great faith in messages from the stars, but were also selectively self-serving about which horoscope to believe. We know this because there is no record of either of them ever missing the big game.

Taped recordings of some of the late French President Francois Mitterrand's astrological consultations were released by his favorite astrologer, Elizabeth Teissier, whose columns of astrologically-based, personal advice are extremely popular.

Teissier said that President Mitterrand had regularly telephoned her between 1989 and 1994 before major decisions. Mitterrand was heard in one tape broadcast by radio France-Info last Saturday, to ask Teissier during the 1991 Gulf conflict for advice about when he should make a public speech.

"You told me there were some days when it was better to speak and others when it was not. Which is the best day to speak? Can you check for me," Mitterrand was heard to say.

Well, what they should have done is elect Miss Teissier President? Then she would have been the only president in history who knew when to keep his/her mouth shut. Mitterrand, on the other hand, could have gone back to asking the wife for permission to speak, like the rest of us do.

It's absolutely true that many great leaders have conducted their affairs of state based on advice from astrologers. Hitler was one and so was Napoleon. Neither of them would ever dare initiate a military campaign without a consultation - and considering how conducive this routine was to their ultimate success, Mitterrand must have made very sure that he wasn't using the same astrologer.

One of the most famous and fatal examples of misinterpretation of astrological advice was the fate of Julius Caesar. Well, okay, he did all right until he was advised not to turn his back on his friends in the Forum. The poor guy thought he was simply being criticized for being aloof. Anyway, He finally got the point - several, in fact. So, I've come to the inescapable conclusion that "Taurus the Bull' is the only sign that really tells it like it is. But just be thankful that you're not the one who has to clean his advice out of your garage

16. MAYBE YOUR DOG
UNDERSTANDS CHINESE

If you are owned by a dog, you will know that the most
wonderful thing about dogs is that they want to make you
happy. That's what dogs live for – well that and whatever it is
they dream about that makes their back leg beat a drum roll on
the carpet.

Have you noticed that look of bafflement in their eyes as
they try to anticipate your wishes? Especially when you say,
"sit" or "heel" or "bath." But they know immediately what your
wishes are when you say "Greetings, Rover; perhaps you would

be partial to ingesting a morsel of succulent sirloin steak." You could say it in Chinese and they would still understand.

At those times our dog, Fifi, will happily do a tap dance or sing an aria from Puccini and she won't be a dumb animal again until she's finished her steak.

On the other hand when she is spread lifelessly across a doorway and I trip over her and break my leg she knows this is not the time to spoil my fun. So she just languishes and snuffles gently to let me know she doesn't mind a bit and to do it again if it will make me happy. After all I do have another leg.

Even when Fifi is lying across a doorway waiting to break a leg, she will immediately respond to a high pitched cry of "kitty, kitty, kitty," by lifting her ears like wings, then wild eyed she will tear madly around the house and, in a final frenzy, throw herself headlong at the front door.

A dog's devotion has nothing at all to do with intelligence. A dog's brain is just one big lump of love and a smattering of "what's for dinner?" They are never quite sure what it will take to make us feed them every day for sitting around doing nothing.

For instance, you and I know that "kitty, kitty, kitty," means go and eat that cat, (Note to cat owners: we would never let her do that – even of it's an especially delicious cat that's been yowling outside the window all night.)

But all Fifi knows is that whenever we repeat something three times in a high-pitched voice she is expected to react in some way. And she has found that throwing herself headlong at the front door is the reaction that pleases us most. Dogs probably discuss us with their friends.

"Hey, prince, what the heck does walkies, walkies, walkies mean?"

"Gee, I've no idea, Fifi. All I know is that every time they say it, I'm dragged out of the house with a rope round my neck before I even get a chance to figure it out. You would think that at least I would get a trial, first. People can be a real pain in the tail, sometimes."

Isn't it strange that we don't mind our dog not having a work ethic? In fact dogs have a strict NO work ethic. We expect nothing from them. And that's what we get. We carry out the most servile and futile tasks for our pet. I mean, we are delighted to put food in a bowl so we can retrieve it later with a scooper from someone's lawn. Why the journey? Why don't we just pick up the food with a scooper and dump in a plastic bag? We wouldn't even have to leave the house.

Fifi has forty two teeth. Two rows of curved incisors help her maintain a firm grip on her prey, while four large, pointed canine teeth tear at it. Then she has sixteen sharp premolars, including the carnassials, which allow her to cut and slice the flesh, while ten powerful grinding molars mean she can chew the non-flesh part of her diet. And all she eats is a bowl of dry dog food.

Dogs can learn to sit, roll over and run away when you call them. But, have you noticed, nobody has ever taught a dog to mow the lawn or clean windows? Even clever little Eddie on Frasier, who has learned to eat caviar from a bowl on the table, is just not smart enough to learn how to take the bowl to the kitchen and wash it.

Right now, I don't like the way Fifi is looking at me and baring her two rows of curved incisors. I think she's wondering if I'm going to put her in a barrel again and tell her to sit in the corner for a bite of steak. She gets real dizzy when I do that and she still doesn't know why.

17. WHY CHICKENS LAY EGGS

For as long as I can remember there has been this controversy over whether animals actually think or just go around instincting about stuff, like "where's my dinner?" Without coherent words or thoughts – like teenagers.

Bur even teenagers don't know that if they look at you with their head cocked to one side and pant a little, they could get a new flea collar and have their tummy rubbed.

It amazes me that after all these years we have yet to admit that animals think. It's quite true that your dog focuses a lot of mental energy on worrying that there may never be another dinner. But, that's what we do too, isn't it? That's why we go to work, for heaven's sake.

Surely, when you are on you way out to work and see your dog stretched on the mat, sighing contentedly, you can't possibly believe this situation evolved by chance. Doesn't it strike you as more than mindless instinct when your cat stays out all night, comes home for breakfast then sleeps all day?

It took several centuries and a great deal of intelligent thinking for dogs and cats to get out of the wobbly vicissitudes of the jungle and into the languorous lassitude of your house. And it's insulting and somewhat condescending to grant that they are as intelligent as we are. They might not like to be reduced to that level.

Okay, go ahead. Just see if you can get out of the jungle and go live with someone who expects nothing of you; attends to your every need and loves you all to bits – even if you use the rug as a rest room.

Dogs are even skilled in psychology. They know very well that if they can make you believe they love you unconditionally and not just when you give them a bone, they will get a bone every time - for loving you unconditionally, you understand. Is that smart or what?

I quite agree that it's difficult to imagine an intelligent chicken. This is mostly because they talk funny. I mean even if super beings arrived from another galaxy and spoke like chickens we would think they were idiots, wouldn't we? Then again, that's what we think of all foreigners who don't talk American proper like what us does.

But chickens are smarter than you think. They know very well that if they don't lay eggs they are heading for barbeque land. So they lay eggs all the time, frantically pushing and straining. No wonder they make funny, strangled sounds. I'm sure I would, too.

It's not likely that unthreatened with barbeque land they would lay so many eggs. I mean, without humans to gather them they would each have about twenty kids every week. No one likes kids that much.

Most of the squawking comes from older hens, prompting frantically: "Lay girls, lay; for Pete's sake squeeze em out; forget maternal instinct, either the kids get eaten for dinner or we do."

The other day I watched a wasp desperately trying to get through my closed patio glass door. Again and again it bashed its little head into the glass. Sure it seems stupid but what would you do if you didn't have a key? Well, eventually, the little varmint had had enough and went off and found an open window.

Now, to be able to determine that it had spent too long on its project that wasp must have been aware of the passing of time. At some point it must have thought, "Okay, that's it. This is a no go. I'm out of here, tout suite." If it were just mindless instinct, surely the little guy would still be trying to break the door down and wouldn't even know why it had a shocking headache.

Okay, mindless instinct could make it try the door in the first place but foiled endeavors require definite decisions which must be arrived at by abstract thought. Well, I've never managed to do that, so I can't help being a little jealous.

So, let your dog have a voice in family discussions some time, okay? You'll notice the crafty devil never once mentions bones, but watch out for the panting and that head cocked to one side. Mindless instinct? Yeah, right.

18. IS LEAD GOOD FOR MOTOR SKILLS?

During our formative years, we older folk had advantages that today's kids don't have. For a start all our water pipes were lead. We were given little lead toy soldiers for Christmas and were told that if we chewed the heads off we should be sure to swallow them only with food. And dad would make jolly remarks about porcelain being susceptible to birdshot – whatever that meant.

Our tea mugs were also lead - just in case we neglected to chew our soldiers' heads off. And to be on the safe side our teaspoons were radioactive uranium.

So we got our uranium supply by teaspoon and our lead by toy soldiers and lead water pipes and lead mugs. Lead was believed to improve our judgment of people and was even claimed to be responsible for our belief that Hitler was just trying to form a marching band.

Inequality was still in vogue so girls didn't get their lead by toy soldiers, or even toy dolls. They were restricted to lead by water pipes. We boys would offer to supplement their supply and gave them a choice between, getting easily lead or getting lead astray. It was probably the effects of chewing uranium spoons that made us think this would work.

Our teachers, whose water also came from lead pipes, cared about our psychological well being. They held parent anger management classes. It's true these meetings always ended in violent fist fights and bloodshed and smashed chairs, but the nuns usually won because they had lead pipes, so that was okay.

The last meeting was later named World War Two and, of course, the fun stopped because there was a shortage of lead.

The army anger management division needed the lead to make bullets, which we sent to the enemy hoping that chewing on them would improve their compassion and generosity of spirit. And it must have worked because pretty soon the enemy was doing the same for us. It was certainly more effective than our failed campaign of "lead astray" and "easily lead", I can tell you.

Do you know that lead pipes are still to be seen in the ruined Italian city of Pompeii? The people of Pompeii obviously knew about the benefits of lead in the water. But, before they could prove it by living a long, healthy life they were wiped out by volcano poisoning, which is quicker but not nearly as much fun as anger management classes.

It's true that, in my youth, medical care providers were very caring. Most of their instruments were made of lead or uranium. Doctors still saved lives, of course. Mostly they did it by staying away from patients. And patients refused to accept house calls. They preferred the doctor's waiting room where, at least they might die of old age before being seen. Some things never change.

Fish, like shark and tuna provided our daily requirements of mercury. Yes, of course, those fish have always provided large doses of this element. There's obviously nothing new about that. I mean if someone today were deliberately supplying the oceans with mercury, surely they would expect a reward for their efforts.

In my view, it's unfair to deprive today's kids of lead in their water, not to mention, lead soldier chew toys. But I suspect that some of them might have found a supplier.

Take rappers, for instance. Their thinking is so concise. Their minds are not fogged by superfluous reasoning. Even their music is admirably economical. I mean, why do we need more than one note for each song. It's wasteful and indecisive.

I've taken the trouble to talk to them, maybe learn something. "Why" they ask, "do your singers go up and down the scale, always searching for the right note?" "For crying out loud," they shriek, "why don't you just pick one and stick to it, like what we do."

Glen Miller drives them mad. They even wrote a song about his band:

"Bunch of crazy ***** people **** belting out **** notes looking for the **** right **** one and never **** finding the **** thing." Well, they're probably right. I mean there must have been a good note they could have used in there somewhere, right?

It's pretty obvious to me that Glen Miller and his band were sadly unleaded – as were Frank Sinatra and Bing Crosby.

Okay, now, I'm going to get some tea in my lead mug and work on word economy. Maybe see if I can think of just one word that would describe rap music. No, not oxymoron, that's too obvious; no, another one... like... let me see, let me see...

19. DOGS ARE NOT GOOD AT PRETENDING

My standard poodle, Fifi, is really my wife's dog because I hardly ever see her. But I have, what you might call, visitation privileges. This means that, when my wife is away for a few days, Fifi and I get to take care of each other.

Because of the absence of a father figure in her life, Fifi has become very feminine. She has picked up all kinds of lovable female behavior from my wife - like biting anyone who leaves the toilet seat up. Okay, Fifi doesn't often use the bathroom herself – well not the toilet – but she wonders why women are not able to lower toilet seats.

She figures that after chaining themselves to railings and getting the vote and stuff, women would be loathe to indicate that there is still something that only men can do, unless it were true.

Fifi can't lower a toilet seat because her thumbs are located halfway up her arm. So, she presumes that women must have a corresponding toilet-seat-lowering disability.

But, of course, some men do, too, don't they? Yet they can be spurred into overcoming their disability by just a few loving words of encouragement.

Fifi and I are buddies. I don't need to worry about her hurting me for leaving the seat up. Oh, sure, she playfully pretends to bite my ankle. And she's getting better at pretending all the time so I hardly limp at all now.

Fifi is an old fashioned female who believes in the ancient code of ladies first (except when crossing a mine field or confronting an intruder) so if you take your eyes off the roast beef for a minute – like to put the toilet seat down – your roast is dragged from the counter and into the yard. And before you can prevent her from being the first to eat, she and the beef are in the pool where all the chlorine gravy is.

She's getting so good at this that we've entered her for the backstroke in the Olympics where she is certain to win a gold medal. I'll bet not many competitors can do the backstroke while holding a leg of beef. Well, not while paddling with their ears, anyway. Maybe it will inspire a new event.

Fifi is quite beautiful – for a dog – and she resents it. She would much rather look like a Pit Bull. So she tries to remedy her condition by leaping into muddy puddles and frowning a lot so that she'll get wrinkles. But all she gets is baths, which, she hates even more than not being the first to eat.

Still, it's beautiful how much my wife and Fifi are beginning to resemble each other. And if it were not for the unconditional love bit they would be very much alike. Sometimes, when Fifi is in one of her exuberant moods, leaping frantically around the room, colliding with walls and furniture, I can see exactly how my wife would look if she had just won the lottery.

And Fifi likes television and is in charge of the remote. She selects a particular station by varying the density of Poodle slobber on the desired button. (Remember where her thumbs are?)

She just loves to watch horses on TV, but she's not really that knowledgeable. I mean, she thinks an equestrian is someone who walks everywhere. And she thinks a pedestrian is a baby doctor. Well she's just a dog. How can she know that it's someone who fixes feet?

Anyway, she watched a show where they were fussing over a Quarter Horse and now she wants to be a quarter poodle. She wonders why they have buffalo quarters and horse quarters but no poodle quarters. Even a poodle penny or a dog dime would do.

But, Fifi and I love each other a lot. We sit on the sofa and hold hands and watch Lassie reruns while Fifi drools over the remote. But even in this she has become more like my wife – no, not the drooling – what I mean is, she never listens to me unless I talk during a movie - and then only so she can tell me to shut up. But, that's better than nothing, right?

Now, this is a secret, okay? Well, I've designed a drool-operated remote control so Fifi can raise and lower the toilet seat while watching television. Of course, I won't be there when my wife stumbles into the family room and tells Fifi that she should never, never again flip the seat while the bathroom is occupied. Okay, so I forgot to tell Fifi about that. I can only hope the little pooch is getting better at pretending to bit ankles.

20. DO IT YOURSELF

In our house my wife is the handyman. She fixes everything. It doesn't necessarily have to be broken; she fixes it anyway. One of the reasons for her industry is that she loves tools. Many years ago she bought a whole bunch of them because the handles were pretty and because the tool shop was the only store open on Christmas day when her credit card was feeling neglected.

Another reason for her need to constantly use her tools is that she hates waste. She just can't bear to have something she owns just sitting there taking up space and doing nothing to justify its existence. I guess I'm her only failure in this respect.

At first, she would prowl around looking for anything broken. Sometimes she would turn to me in frustration and say "can't you break something? If you really loved me you'd break something that can only be fixed with a two inch wrench and a number six Philips head screwdriver with a yellow handle."

So just to please her I would go and drain all the oil from her car and tamper with the brake fluid. How was I to know that the bodywork would be so badly damaged? And would you believe she tried to blame me just because I forgot to tell her about the brake fluid. There's no pleasing some people.

Of course, it's not all fun and games. There is a down side to all of this too. I guess one of the things that really bugs me is when the plumber calls and leaves desperate messages asking her to fix his pipes or unblock his drains. And, sometimes, during a storm, when the entire South Valley is blacked out, the power company will call asking what the trouble is and when it will be fixed and can we lend them a 40-watt bulb for the nuclear power station.

But what's really sad is that even the dog is forbidden to sit around not justifying her existence. Well, I can tell you, once you've seen a dog being forced to chew leaves and twigs to make mulch for the garden; you're not likely to forget it in a hurry. Especially the whimpering.

And the amazing thing is that my wife can't understand why the poor beast keeps running away. But, even she has to admit that the only time our wild eyed canine was actually found thumbing rides on the freeway was after she had seen a book on "do it yourself neutering" left lying about near the tool chest. Somehow I don't think there are too many of us who would hang around to find out if the tools had pretty handles.

One of the problems is that the whole thing is self perpetuating. She starts on a job - say repairing a back hoe in the front yard while she's waiting for her nails to dry - then discovers that she needs to buy more tools to complete the job. So it's not surprising that she has the most comprehensive collection of tools outside of General Motors. And what's more the handles are prettier.

But, I guess the most frightening day of my life was when she brought home a chain saw. Well, I almost ran away with the dog but all my shoes were dismantled, being repaired, and I had no idea how to put the engine back in my car. It's something that will always haunt my dreams. There she stood, grimly brandishing her chain saw and looking around belligerently, like a presidential aide visiting the oval office for a friendly chat with Bill.

Still, to be fair, I think that a lot of her enthusiasm is due to the paternal influences of her formative years. You see, her father built the house they lived in with his own hands. All of it; the walls, the pipes, and the wiring.

And he didn't have anywhere near the tools that we have - even if you only count the ones on top of the television. I guess he would be pleased because we all want our kids to have more than we had, don't we?

In fact it's strange that it took her so long to discover her penchant for plumbing, plastering and painting; especially when you consider that when she was told, as a youngster, that her place was in the kitchen, her father meant that she should be installing the waste disposal unit or repairing the fridge.

On the other hand my own father was averse to all kinds of manual labor including the garden. He thought that a Rototiller was a member of some obscure religious sect; and I'm I still not sure if he wrong about that.

Anyway, last week my wife repaired the thermostat for the air conditioning unit. It has just three wires and is not much bigger that a deck of cards. Originally It was held to the wall by two tiny screws, but it wasn't too long before it was hanging on desperately by one wire and the hall was wall to wall tools - including pipe wrenches.

At her feet, the chain saw bared its teeth and smiled ominously, knowing that it's time would surely come. Well, she finally got the thermostat working, but now it alerts the police station and the FBI whenever the temperature falls below sixty. Still, not to worry; tomorrow we'll go and buy some more tools. Or maybe I'll just fix it with the Rototiller.

21. NO LEFT ARM LEFT, RIGHT?

It seems that people from Laragne in the southern Alpine region of France are bred tough. Nothing you can do can hurt them. This is because they have no idea it hurts until their mother points it out to them. Yes, that hurts," she will say. "You can go outside and yell right after you get the piano off your foot."

But the people are not silly. Naturally, if a mother notices that her teenage son has fewer fingers after chopping wood than he had before, she doesn't tell him it hurts until after he's finished his piano practice. Like any mother, she knows very well that he will use any little excuse to shirk his duties

On the bright side she is happy that it will certainly cut down on his nail biting. "Ah well, every cloud has a silver lining" she will say. They are very strong on philosophy in Laragne. They are also very strong on drinking huge quantities of red wine and waking up in the cow shed after hours of feeling no pain at all.

Anyway, last week, Olivier Faure a 21-year-old man from Laragne was hit by a car and knocked off his moped in the village of Upaix. The driver, noticing that Olivier was from Laragne, left the scene without telling the young man that being knocked off a moped hurts. He thought it best to let Olivier's mother break the news to him.

When the driver fled the scene, Olivier, with his moped totaled, set off to walk the 10km to his home before getting a lift from a passing motorist. When he finally arrived his mother gave him his dinner and was surprised to see that he was having trouble cutting his meat. This was strange, because kids from

Laragne are known to be advanced beyond their years. In fact Olivier had been feeding himself without help from his mom since he was nineteen.

Anyway, three hours later, exhausted from swallowing an uncut three pound steak, he slipped his jacket off because, being smart, he had discovered that it was difficult to lower his suspenders without doing so. Well, his mother was relieved to discover that his left arm was missing and that he wasn't really too dumb to cut his meat after all. He was just left arm challenged.

"Where's your left arm?" she said casually. "I know you had it when you left because you tied your boot laces." Well, it was obvious that he was as surprised as she was; and then the truth dawned. "Gee mom," He said. "I must have lost it when that car hit me."

"Why didn't you bring it home?" she said angrily. And she cuffed him on the left side of his head because now, with his arm missing, she knew he couldn't defend himself.

Later, they were both pleased to learn that the police had found the missing limb by the side of the road. You were tres tres lucky" said the police inspector to the boy's mom. "It was beaucoup fortunate that it was a part of his body that had fingerprints at the end of it." "que sera, sera and deja vu all over again," answered Olivier's mom, philosophically. She was French, you see.

After proof of ownership had been established, the arm was packed in ice and flown together with its owner to Marseille, where it was sewn back on. The surgeon refused to give Olivier anesthetic, based on the premise that if he didn't feel the thing coming off he wasn't likely to feel it being put back. "Makes sense to me," said Olivier's mom." Well it wasn't her arm, was it?

It wasn't long before a local driver was arrested and charged with arm robbery. He wept and insisted that he would have rescued the arm from the ditch and hosed it down, had he not been running late for happy hour. The judged nodded sympathetically. "Mai oui," he said. (He was French too.) "Life is like a cup of tea." He was also strong on Philosophy; and, running late for happy hour himself, felt he would have done the same thing, and left the arm in the ditch.

In mitigation, the offending motorist told the court that he had, in fact, saved Olivier's life. If the young man had continued on his way, un-hindered, he would have run into a dead cow, three sheep and a huge farmer strewn across the road where the motorist had hit them just before he ran into Olivier.

Luckily, the motorist had a smart lawyer. "I'll fight for you," he said with a steely look in his eye. Then, ducked behind the accused as they left the court for lunch. Well, maybe the victim's family were vengeful people, and being well aware of the people's right to bear left arms he preferred to hang on to his own until after the meat course.

22. *SLUG SNAILS AND NAIL SLUGS*

It's true I could never be accused of doing great things to improve the lot of mankind, but at least I know how to grow a lettuce. You will have noticed that slugs and snails are not able to do this. If they were they wouldn't need to eat mine. Would they?

Oh, I know that however hard I try I will never be able to slither across the dirt at midnight leaving a slimy trail. Still, I'm told I got pretty close to it on the lawn at the church bazaar fundraiser after sampling Mrs. Nockembak's dandelion wine. But I've never managed to do it again. For one thing, Mrs. Nockembak wouldn't give me her address. But no slug or snail has ever got pretty close to growing a lettuce, has it?

Seriously, now, if you were in charge of the flood would you take two of everything? Even slugs and snails? Well, I think it was a mistake. All it did was get them on a cruise to my garden to eat my lettuce.

The ark is probably where the animals learned that they didn't have to grow their own food. We superior beings who had been granted dominion over all the animals would do it for them.

That's also where we superior beings learned how to use pooper-scoopers and change kitty litter. I guess the snails and slugs could be forgiven for thinking that if we didn't mind doing all that stuff we wouldn't be too put out about a little thing like having our lettuce eaten.

And what about the dreaded nightly ark calls for arms and necks to feed thousands of mosquitoes. Oh yes, I know all the animals started out as only one of each sex but the mosquitoes were the first to find out why.

Poor old Noah and the missus must have been running around like crazy trying to keep the slugs and snails from eating the lettuce they were growing for the lions. I mean, when there are only two antelopes left, it's time to get creative. Especially since it was already too late to save the unicorns.

There must have been times when Noah stood on the deck looking for icebergs – hoping.

The other worrying thing is that since Noah went to all the trouble to save the slugs and snails, is it right for me to kill them off? And, if so, should it be one at a time or two by two? Well, the truth is they can't be killed off. Not with slug bait, anyway.

Slug bait will kill your lettuce quickly enough but that's pointless because you have slugs and snails to do that for you, so why bother?

Sure if you stay in the yard with a flashlight all night you can stomp on them before they reach your lettuce. Stomping is pretty foolproof for most things. Okay, not minefields. The trouble is that snails and slugs are smarter than we are. If they weren't we would be eating their lettuce instead of the other way around, wouldn't we?

What they do is come out of their holes one at a time starting around midnight. So you stomp that one and then you have to wait 2 hours for the next one to hurry out for its turn.

After a few hours you may decide to eat all the lettuce yourself and go to bed. That's what people who are smarter than slugs and snails do. You've already guessed that I'm not one of them, haven't you?

You would do well to think about all this when you see those 200 heads of lettuce waiting for you in the produce department at Save Mart.

But all is not lost. I've just read a book, which tells me where snails and slugs hide when they're not eating my lettuce. Seems I can easily wipe them out by knocking down all my fences, tearing up my deck boards and taking a sledge to the water meter. I don't need to chop down all the trees, just the ones with bark and leaves. Oh, and as I have to go down to the hardware store for dynamite and a bulldozer, I think I'll just drop into Save Mart for some lettuce - instead.

23. STIR YOURSELF AT TEA TIME

The big question is should a man, who is sitting comfortably in his chair doing nothing but wait for someone to stir his tea, be expected to get his own dinner? Since when has the master of the house been required to make concessions that could severely damage his maleness? Okay, there are probably a few women out there who could think of more creative ways to damage it.

But can a wife ever be justified in putting her husband to such hazardous inconvenience just because she happens to be engaged in decorating their ten-room house when he wants his dinner?

So the man dialed 999, which is English for 911 and, like its American counterpart is used for such emergencies as rescuing a drowning goldfish from the aquarium and getting a message to the vicar that he should pull the arrow out of the guy's back before he buries him. Serious stuff like that.

Anyway, he was in a masculine fury and demanded that the police either send someone to get his dinner or someone to do the decorating. "I'm sorry," said the police officer, "but our only female police person is cleaning the captain's shoes, she can't get there until after dinner time."

"But what am I supposed to do?" cried the guy, sounding more like Britney Spears every minute. "Don't you see, she left me..."

"She left you?" said the cop.

"I wish you would stop interrupting," cried the man, getting a sudden urge to pull the cop's hair. "I said she left me with two salmon sandwiches what was left over from last night and I'm sat in this chair here and she's out there decorating."

Then to show more clearly that he was not an ignoramus but an educated guy to be reckoned with, he said, "And she won't put no food on or nothing for nobody." Well that got the cop's attention. Cops in this little country town in Somerset, South West England, don't come across too many people who can speak Lithuanian.

At this point the female operator interrupted, saying, "I'm sorry but I really can't take this. It's not an emergency just because your wife won't give you anything to eat. My husband tried that last week.

"But the poor guy must be starving by now."

"Oh no, he's the one the vicar buried with an arrow in his back. Suicide by bow and arrow," she said," stifling a sob - or something.

Well, men, I know it's not fair, but take care. Now that women have the vote you may soon be expected to stir your own tea. So don't make them mad, okay?

In Mexico City, the authorities have urged women to strike and put down their mops and pans to mark international domestic workers day. Thousands of men were chagrined by this emasculating move and wanted to start their own workers day tradition but, only two guys qualified as workers, and they were in the yard burying their bows and arrows.

Gabriella Delgado, of the women's institute, thinks that household tasks should be divided equally between men and women. See, I told you not to make them mad.

But it's not just England and Mexico where men are having problems demanding their rights. One man in Germany ignored my warning.

His wife clubbed him to the floor with his ashtray (well, he had been warned that smoking was dangerous) then she used his underwear as an offensive weapon to choke him. But she insisted that his long johns had actually been offensive for years and had strangled him without any assistance from her at all.

Anyway, I don't know about you, but I'm going to get dinner ready before that darned dog digs up my bow and arrow again.

24. WHAT IS THAT?

Deep down in your soul, is there a frustrated artist struggling to get out? When you look at a painting do you know you could do better if you had the time?

And what about that novel? It's so frustrating. You know it would be a best seller if only you had time to stop doing the things that are stopping you from starting. Is that clear to you? If it is, please let me know so that I can start doing it too.

I must confess that I too have been bitten by the artist bug and feel it my duty to warn you of the pitfalls. After looking at the Sistine Chapel ceiling I decided to take up painting. Well, it looked so easy. All I would need to do the same thing to Westminster Abby would be a very long brush and a note from the queen to say it was okay. But I decided to start with art classes.

Well, when I turned up at art school people were standing at easels trying to look like Michelangelo, and, I suspect, some of them had actually been around at the time to help Mike with the Sistine Chapel.

But, after a five-minute lesson I thought I should start closer to the ground, so I painted a picture of the dog

This is because she doesn't move much, unless I'm being attacked, then she runs away.

Well, my first mistake was hanging the picture on the wall where people could actually see it. "That's a nasty stain on your wallpaper," some would say, sympathetically. Others pretended they hadn't seen it so they wouldn't be forced to use bad language. So I fitted a searchlight against the opposite wall to bring out the colors. When visitors arrived they had to face the picture or be blinded by the light.

One guest was fascinated by the picture. "Why are you lighting up a picture of Alcatraz?" he asked. "Did someone escape?" Well, I must say, the dog caught on quickly and, loyal as ever, began assuming grotesque poses trying desperately to look like Alcatraz. But by then my guest had decided to risk blindness by staring into the light

My advice to budding artists is, store your pictures in the attic and when you're dead you will be famous. It happens a lot.

Discriminating art lovers will say, "hey, that's a really good picture of Alcatraz for a dead person, let's bury it with him," and other complimentary stuff like that. Be patient. Your day will come.

But it's a tough business all round, so I'm going to help you out with a few tips. What a lot of painters have started to do is show their paintings before they are finished. So when someone looks over your shoulder and says, "Hey, if that thing didn't have a personality it would look just like Al Gore, you quickly paint out the personality. You get the picture?

Don't tell anyone but that's how the Mona Lisa became inscrutable. Someone said, "Hey Leonardo I'd like to buy that picture but I can't decide if I like Lisa laughing or scowling," So, with an inscrutable flourish Leonardo compromised. Well, you've got to sell the stuff.

Then there's my friend Vincent, who was proudly showing his unfinished picture and trying to decide what it was when someone said, "what is it?

"What does it look like," Vincent explained, picking up the pencil that he had tried to put on his ear. The art critic stepped back, knocking over a vase of unrealistic plastic sunflowers. "Well," he said, "if it were wearing a lampshade and a sequined Elvis Presley suit it would look just like the pope."

Today, Vincent is one of the most up and coming excommunicated painters in Latvia.

So I was busy with my welder creating some modern art from pieces I had picked up at a garage sale, and someone said, "what is it?"

"What does it look like?" I explained.

"Well, it looks like a garage sale," he grinned. And, quick as a flash, I said, "that's what it is, and while you're here would you like to buy a painting of Alcatraz?"

Well, I imagine you've got the idea by now – or do I have to draw you a picture?

25. WHAT'S IN A NAME?

Strange that Johnny Cash should have chosen Folsom prison as a venue for venting his wrath at being called "Sue". Folsom is not the place for a guy who doesn't like to tempt providence, especially if he is a guy named Sue. It's not the place for a girl named Sue, either, but that's another song.

Some guys named Sue have made the mistake of believing it would be wiser if they were a little aloof. But saying, "please call me Susan until we know each other better" has always been a huge failure in Folsom.

You are probably aware that naming a boy Kanae in Japan is about the same as calling him Sue in America.

In Tokyo, a judge sentenced, Kaname Yoshida to 14 years in prison for stabbing his father who named him Kanae, a feminine sounding name, which has "a phonetically feminine ending." Kanea changed it to Kaname in 1976.

His dad could never understand what the fuss was about. Well, of course not. I mean, when introduced to someone, he didn't constantly have to make a snap decision on whether to bow or curtsy, did he?

Kaname, an unemployed carpenter, looked quite cheerful when sentenced. But a friend blamed himself for not seeing the significance in Kaname's clenched jawed renditions of "If I had a hammer," whenever Kaname was with his dad. "I just thought, so what? The guy's a carpenter isn't he?" said the friend.

As it turns out, Yoshida stabbed his father so, obviously, he never did manage to get hold of a hammer. But his revenge seems a bit harsh just for having to live with an ending that was phonetically feminine.

I mean, no one can tell me that after that first stab the old man wasn't backing away, screaming, "Okay, okay. I'll call you George, or Ernie, ow, ow, that's enough, Stud, that's it, Bill." Obviously he didn't have time to hit on the boy's favorite name, but you can bet he suspected it wasn't Sue.

Judge Kenichi Hiruma of the district court in Tochiga state announced the ruling on Thursday. The Defendant's conduct is brutal and leaves no room for a pardon," he wrote in his ruling.

Well it's all very well for the judge to be judgmental. He wasn't called Sue, was he? But there is a rumor that he changed his mind about calling his own new son, Sylvia, Hyacinth. It wouldn't have made a very good song, anyway, would it?

I can't help wondering what the reaction will be if Johnny Cash ever visits Kaname's jail and sings his famous song. I guess Johnny would be quite safe as long as Kaname hadn't found a hammer yet.

In the song's lyrics the father explains his reason for naming his son Sue, with the words: "Son, this world is rough, and if a man's gonna make it he's gotta be tough."

Well, I guess, if that's the reason John Wayne was named "Marion," (Morrison) it worked. I mean can you imagine some guy saying, "Hey, come here, Marion darlin?" to John Wayne. What I mean is, can you imagine him saying it twice?

And the thing is that John Wayne never thought about changing his name until, as a prop boy, moving furniture on the set, he was spotted by renowned director, Raoul Walsh.

Walsh didn't think a romantic lead tough guy should be called Marion Morrison. John once said he didn't mind being called John Wayne as long as they paid him for pretending to act.

I wonder if anyone would have heard of John Wayne today, had he kept his original name. Is a name so important? I guess it is. I can't imagine "True Grit" starring, "Hyacinth Honey-Love Morrison. Can't you just hear the growl? "That'll be the day.

Although my own family had a funny last name, we were all given ordinary first names. My Dad was named Michael, and everyone called him Mick. Naturally, the guys called my mother, Mrs. Mick. Wouldn't that make today's ladies grip the carpet with their toes? I don't know why my Mom didn't sue them. No not sue; I mean, Sue, as in give them a phonetically feminine ending.

26. WHY DOGS ACT CRAZY

You have probably wondered why all dogs sometimes act a little crazy. Me too. So I've done some research. It seems that dogs have been living with humans for over 10,000 years? No, that's not the official explanation of why all dogs act crazy, but it makes you wonder, doesn't it?

Anyway, 10,000 years ago was just about the end of the human, stone age. I guess you could say it was the beginning of the canine bone age, a period, which has been largely ignored by Paleontologists.

And possibly, one of the reasons it was never documented is because it could easily have been the end of Paleontology, as we know it. Dogs never change, you see. They are just dogs. There would have been nothing new to document for 10,000 years.

Humans, however, have evolved in all kinds of bizarre ways. From peaceful cave dwellers to savages to barbarians to republicans, to... Well, okay, maybe we should have stopped at peaceful cave dwellers.

If you think this makes you smarter than your dog, think again. I mean, which one of you says stuff like, "Oh gosh darn it, I'm late for work again," and which says, "woof, woof where's my dinner, I'm late for sleeping till noon."

And when your dog chases its tail you probably laugh and call it a silly darling? But, you see, dogs noticed long ago that none of the animals their masters ate for dinner chased its tail. It was clear that no human could bring himself to eat any creature that chases its tail. And that's because it's cute. All animals need cute to survive around humans. Even humans need cute to survive around humans.

But, cute aside, if early humans ate their dog they would never know if it could actually catch its tail. I mean that thing goes around real fast, doesn't it? And being human, we are all saddled with this profound intellectual depth, which prevents us from not caring one way or the other.

Even savages liked to watch mysteries being solved. Stuff like "CSI Tail Watch," "To Catch a Tail," "Paw and Order." You will notice that no dog ever makes the mistake of actually catching the thing.

In old time Iraq, humans would play games with their dogs called "Find the Weapons" "Come on boy, Find those weapons," they would cry. But, it was all in fun. They knew deep down that if the dogs really did have weapons of mass destruction buried, they would have had the humans chasing their tails instead of the other way around.

Over the years, dogs have been used to hunt for food, herd animals, pull carts, perform rescues, and apprehend lawbreakers.

But from personal experience, I should admit that none of this stuff applies to poodles called, Fifi. If I mention work she immediately develops a shocking cough and goes to bed. The sources for my research on dog stuff made no mention of Fifi at all. Just like your dog, she is unique and can't be categorized together with the other canine riff-raff

When Fifi appears to be chasing her tail, It's not for silly reasons like cute. She simply believes that her tail is chasing her. And Fifi's tail is special because I'm pretty sure that's where she keeps her brain.

Naturally, when she wags her tail it makes her dizzy. So when she is happy she just wags her eyes from side to side, back and forth, back and forth. She doesn't get dizzy at all but the rest of us tend to fall over after a few minutes of watching her being happy

It seems that, before you buy a puppy, it's useful to give the little guy a temperament test to see if it gets mad at you. One of the tests involves taking the pup under your arm, squeezing and manipulating the webbing between the toes. If the response is a strange howling sound that starts other dogs digging for weapons, you know your new dog will be a valuable member of a bagpipes band. Luckily for you, most of those are in Scotland.

The trouble with Fifi's temperament is that I can never tell when she's lying. Well, all dogs look guilty when they wag their eyes don't they? Especially when they have their brain tucked between their legs.

27. IT'S THE LAW

If you live in Iowa and your horse eats a fire hydrant while you are selling tickets to see a one-armed piano player, you're in trouble. It's against the law; well it's against two laws actually.

But it's perfectly legal to invite people to see the one-armed piano player so long as you don't charge admission - no, not even half price.

Iowa also has a law that firemen are required to practice for fifteen minutes before attending a fire. Practice? Well, why don't they practice on the house that's on fire, for heaven's sake?

My advice to any Iowa fireman who feels the need to flee this dubious decree is: don't go to St. Louis, Missouri. In St Louis, it's illegal for a fireman to rescue a woman in a nightgown. Don't you think that's ridiculous? What if the fireman has just bought a new night gown and the station sergeant says he looks good in it; why shouldn't he wear it to the fire?

The trouble with Missouri is that it has other laws too, such as, it's forbidden for women to wear hats that might frighten timid persons, children, or animals. So if a timid person is scared by an illegal meeting of millinery militants, what can he do to calm his timid nerves? Well, I'll tell you what he can't do; He can't sit on the curb of a city street and drink beer from a bucket. It's illegal – in spite of another Missouri law that considers drunkenness an "Inalienable Right."

But it's not just Missouri that seems to be concerned with illicit headgear. In Fargo, North Dakota, "One may be jailed for wearing a hat while dancing." And Lang, in Kansas forbids you to ride a mule down Main Street in August unless the animal is wearing a straw hat.

Still, it seems to me that this law is open to interpretation; must it be only a straw hat or is it all right for the little critter to wear a homburg or a bowler, or maybe flaunt a Fred Astaire Topper – even though it would be illegal to wear it while dancing. Someone once said that the law is an ass. Perhaps it should have been, "The law is an ass wearing a straw hat."

Be careful if you go to Illinois. It's illegal to speak English. The officially recognized language is American. Strangely enough, this is a distinction the English have been making for years. Still, it pales beside another state law that decrees, "It's illegal to fish in your pajamas. I mean what could you possibly have swimming around in your pajamas that you would want to catch with a rod and line?

And in Chicago you could be clapped in irons for taking your French Poodle to the opera. Unfortunately, the poor pooch wouldn't be any better off if you took her to Menominee, Michigan, where it's illegal to walk backwards on First Street with a pickle in your mouth. Well, what kind of life would that be for the little tike? It wouldn't be easy to sing opera without a pickle in her mouth, would it – or to recite doggerel, for that matter.

The good thing about civil laws is that companies can issue disclaimers to protect themselves against being sued. But the disclaimers are sometimes just as weird as the laws.

95

A container of hair styling mousse warns, "Avoid fire and flame until hair is thoroughly dry." Okay, once your hair is dry, you may set fire to as often as you like. If it gets out of control the fire brigade will save you - unless you're in Iowa where you'll have to wait fifteen minutes while they practice on someone else.

It's scary to think that it's probably the result of someone forgetting to do this that prompted a baby- stroller manufacturer to warn: "Always remove the baby before folding the stroller."

Imagine a warning at the meat counter that "tongue comes from an animal's mouth." Well I know I wouldn't want to eat something that comes from an animal's mouth. Give me an egg any day.

Who can blame airlines for warning that aircraft sometimes collide with mountains at six hundred miles an hour. But, never mind; sue them anyway. I mean, you have the advantage because, unlike the Airline, you don't have to pay your lawyer unless you win.

Whoops, now my darned horse is trying to eat a fire hydrant. I better take off his straw hat before he starts to dance with a one-armed piano player with a pickle in his mouth. It's probably against the law.

28. HUMPHREY BOGART'S HAT

The modern custom of switching off our brain every evening and indulging in something that doesn't require its use is nothing new. We did it long before television. In fact we needed to do it more in the old days because life itself seemed infinitely better if we found ways to not think about it too much. But as you've often heard, we were happy. And now you know why.

When someone else was reading the family book and we were tired of staring at each other, it was easier to shut down intelligent and rational thought than it is today.

Without the diversion of television we were more skilled at functioning just on screen saver and could be brought back to our normal semi comatose state at a shout of "dinners ready," or "the baby's on fire."

If we should accidentally shut down altogether, my mother was always happy to boot us up again - and they were hobnailed and hard to ignore. But soon family life was threatened by the advent of new fangled wireless sets.

My father, once an avid reader of the racing page, would now sit with his ear glued to one of those old fashioned radios shaped like a Norman arch, (the radio, not my father.) And instead of his lifelong intellectual pursuit of studying form he would listen to scary stories like, "the man in black" and "Sexton Blake," his eyes focused on some seemingly far distant, unattainable object beyond his comprehension - my mother again.

In those days it was a common belief that radio was responsible for the crumbling of civilized society. Some blamed the radio for promoting cigarettes by using the sound effects of rain on Humphrey Bogart's hat.

And there was never any doubt that Sexton Blake was responsible for World War 11. Well, he knew nothing of political correctness, you see, and called his sidekick, who was curly, "Curly" and a blonde friend "Blondie." World War 11 was the only way to stop the rot and it was worth it.

Of course there was no Internet to divert us - unless you want to count a yelled conversation from our window to a receiving window across the road. Naturally, you couldn't call it a chat room because you didn't actually have to be in the room across the road to join in the chat, anywhere in the street was just fine.

Sometimes it was even interactive. Someone would send a message in the shape of a heavy flowerpot hurled at a deserving neighbor. "Say it with flowerpots" was one of our old fashioned valentine's day suggestions to help win the heart of a recalcitrant loved one. Today, of course, they've edited the wording and ruined the impact.

While we are probably justified in lamenting the decline of the reading habit, many of us like to give the impression that the valuable time we once spent reading in the old days is now being wasted by the young in watching television.

But reading was never the addiction that television is today. No one ever said, "I'm worried. Young Johnny fell asleep in front of the book again last night."

No one ever answered, "Well you shouldn't let him have his own book in his room;" it will give him all sorts of unrealistic ideas like jousting at windmills."

Sometimes we were confused by mixed messages. One kid in our street took out a book about ancient philosophers from the library; then went to see a Walt Disney movie. This is how we learned that Plato was Mickey Mouse's dog.

And for weeks we contemplated with horror the terrible mess Helen's face must have been after she had launched a thousand ships with it. But, of course, it was probably cheaper than a thousand bottles of Champagne, so it was okay.

Unlike today's kids, we were never bored. We each had our interesting hobbies. I still cherish the precious times our canary and I spent trying to stare each other down, hour after wonderful hour until one, or both of us, fell to the ground in a coma with our feet twitching in the air. Stimulating stuff.

99

But, getting back to the joys of reading as compared to the mindless stimulation of some television programs, there is no way we old fashioned kids would have watched television, even if it had been invented. And if you believe that, it's a further indication of the damage that watching television can do to the mind.

But, I must admit that by the time I was twelve I had become an avid reader. Still am. However, there are some authors that while regarded as commendable, can be just as mind numbing as Sexton Blake. Trying to read three pages of Chaucer without sobbing is only marginally easier than contemplating the cover of Rudolph Bing's 5,000 nights at the opera, for ten seconds without nodding off. But I would still rather have just those two books than no books at all. So I guess I'm addicted.

Naturally, nothing can be as much fun as staring down a canary or listening to the rain on Humphrey Bogart's hat but hey, they were the good old days.

29. THE LUMP

If my wife hadn't noticed my lump none of this stuff would have happened. For a start we would never have gone on vacation. I was minding my own business at the time, which is a luxury my wife has never allowed herself. "You've got a lump on your neck," she said. "People only get lumps when they are worn out and need a vacation." She staggered a little and treated herself to a rapid examination. "I'm surprised I haven't got one myself," she said.

But as usual there were one or two obstacles to overcome before I could take my lump on vacation. For a start, we had no money. Also, the kids had got to that awkward stage where they wanted to eat three times a week. Well, what can you do with spoilt kids?

Still, we had a car, which was very unusual in those days. True, we could only keep it for a week, or until the Vicar decided to check his garage - whichever came first. It was a 1935 Austin Seven about the size of a shopping cart, and the difficult part was to get it going - and after that, to make it stop.

Those of you who have never used a starting handle will think I'm making this up, but I'm not. You see, sometimes, as you give the handle a sharp, clockwise crank, the engine will fire briefly and stop. But not before the steel handle kicks back in the opposite direction and breaks your thumb. This makes it very difficult if the car absolutely refuses to start and you need to hitch a lift. You quickly become aware that there is no substitute for the thumb. It's so unambiguous. It says "Please pick me up and save my life." While any other digit could be interpreted as "I hate you so please run me down and leave me for dead."

After all, we only remain supreme custodians of the earth because there is no such thing as an opposable finger. This is why monkeys don't drive.

So, because his thumb is halfway up his arm and out of harms way, I offered the dog a turn with the starting handle, but he took a turn round the block instead. Still he did show there were no hard feelings by marking the handle as part of his territory.

It was thoughtful of him to take the trouble but I did feel sorry for my wife having to grapple with the slippery, smelly handle. Having your thumb broken is bad enough without needing to resist the impulse to shove it into your mouth to ease the pain.

Anyway, eventually we set off in a cloud of pollution. Two kids, a wife, a man, and a lump. Our concept of distance was different in those days. The little seaside town of "Wallow in the Marsh" was only 10 miles away but it took us eighteen hours to get there. Anyone who is surprised by this has never navigated the twists and turns of the old English country lane called the English Channel Freeway.

It was our wonderful roads that saved us during the war. They were the reason that Hitler never invaded. He knew he would be a very old Nazi before his Panzers reached London, which was 200 miles away. So, of course he went east to Moscow, which was only 3000 miles away through ten-foot snowdrifts and much easier to negotiate.

Well, we had great fun as we bumped along in a carbon monoxide fog. At least we knew the kids were fine because the smoke wasn't that awful, second hand stuff you read about.

Our smoke came straight from the engine with just a little detour through the floor. And as we went on our merry way we sang happy songs with the kiddies. "The people on the bus go cough cough choke, cough cough choke," and so on.

To this day the kids have never forgotten that trip. The memory makes them so emotional that they prefer not to talk about it.

We waited until the second kid had thrown up before we stopped for tea because it would have been wasteful, to have them throw up after I had spent 25 cents on dinner. And, being spoilt, they would probably want to eat again within a couple of days or so.

Anyway, soon the vacation was over and, I must say the kids seemed glad we were all crushed together in our own little room again. They had missed the familiar sound of the tap dripping in the corner. And now with the dog, under the sink whimpering for water - even though we had only been gone for a week - it was even more heartwarming. That dog was becoming as spoilt as the kids.

So when the doctor saw the results of the test he looked grave and, in a wonderful display of professional expertise earned by years in medical school said, "You have a lump." "Thank you for being honest with me, doctor," I said. "I suspected it might be something like that.

Then in his usual somber yet reassuring clinical tones that, like the Mona Lisa's smile, can cover all possible contingencies, he said it could easily be an insect bite and would go away if I lent him the vicar's car for his vacation. Well I felt I should explain about the starting handle that the dog had marked as his territory. But he smiled and said, "Oh, that's okay, my wife needs to stop sucking her thumb anyway.

30. DISEASE MORE FUN THAN CURE

If you are experiencing signs of encroaching old age but think you can't do anything about them, you're probably right. But don't give up. There may be a glimmer of hope yet.

Those of us who are looking for this glimmer will remember when there was always a gaily-painted wagon at the fair where a "doctor" offered elixirs to cure all ills. "Roll up, roll up ladies and gents," he would cry. "This little bottle of Amazonian cholera water will cure the Vapors and the Ague and Winkle pickers' gout."

And, you know, he was right. I mean, when was the last time you came across those afflictions – okay, I mean except for winkle pickers gout?

The point is this medicine man never really went away. He just left the fair and hitched his wagon to your television. You may have missed him because he only appears about 48 times during commercial breaks - when many of us are in the bathroom putting ointment on something that, in the old days, could have been cured by splashing it with Amazonian cholera water.

These television commercials try to prove that there are more ways to cure stuff than Amazonian cholera water, which is now in short supply owing to the adverse effects of antibiotics on the active ingredients.

Now, you are assured that after taking only one headache pill you will suddenly be skiing up Mount Everest, dancing all night (providing you don't have winkle pickers gout) and skydiving from the space station. You will actually see 90-year-old amputees doing these things right there on your TV, which never lies.

Of course they admit the pill has a few minor side effects like diarrhea, convulsions, narcolepsy and baggy pants. And, oh yes, it will give you a headache even though you already have one of those.

Buy one get one free, right? And, just think, if you were lucky enough to already have diarrhea you could double your... Anyway, it sounds too good to be true, right?

There are even instant-cure Myopia pills with an instant diagnosis of your eye condition: If you can read the small print that says they give you diarrhea you don't need them.

Now, men can even take pills that will make them more attractive to the ladies. But, the commercial warns that, if you have suppurating toe fungus, infected earwax, eye pus and bloody sputum, you should first ask your doctor for a blood test to make sure the pills won't give you any nasty afflictions that might make you unattractive.

Somehow I don't think the pills are going to do it for these guys - unless they cause myopia and they can get the ladies to take them before the first date.

At one time I tried to regain my lost vigor by riding a stationary bike. I had one in the garage. It was screwed to the floor. It was as stationary as it could get. Even so, my wife would still ask where I was going when I got on it. You may prefer to just take a pill.

Anyway, according to anti-aging experts, if you want to look younger you need to make your lips thicker. To do this, you must learn to whistle. They say you can practice as you walk or wait for a bus or ride in the elevator. Wherever you go, just keep whistling. People will soon be forcing money on you to pay for lip-thickening plastic surgery just to make you stop. So either way you get to feel good.

The report also says that subtle changes can occur in your ears that make them look older. The remedy is to wiggle them. At first the movement may seem relatively slight, but in time you can develop more speed. However, an 80-year-old woman who started the exercises a month ago was last seen over Peru at 30 thousand feet. So wiggle slowly or always carry your passport, okay?

The other thing is posture. To improve it you need to stand with your back against a wall pressing the base of your skull against it as close as you can get. But don't whistle, okay? - especially if there are a couple of guys with violin cases nearby. The temptation could be too much while you are standing against a wall.

So, I figured I'd go to a fitness center and make my body more muscular and attractive and, maybe get to throw away those myopia pills.

Anyway, when I took off my shirt the trainer laughed and said if bodies don't have any lumps, he can't make them bigger and stronger. But, he added, there is a lump pill that might give me some. Okay, sounds promising. But first I better make sure the side effects don't include thin lips or stationary ears.

31. YELLOW CATS

There are so many wonderful things about France. I mean, what could be more wonderful than those long, thin, crusty loaves of bread called baguette? But then, they go and spoil it all, with the language.

Louise XVI invented it as a secret code so that the revolutionaries wouldn't be able to understand each other and demand long crusty bread instead of cake.

Unfortunately, the only word that caught on with everybody was Guillotine, which everyone understood perfectly.

This was particularly unfortunate for the accused aristocrats because the frenzied mob didn't understand words like, "take my wife, not me. She was the one who raped and pillaged your village, please, please, I'm innocent." and other aristocratic gallantries.

No, what the mob heard was, "Spare my dear wife and please chop off my head instead," and, "It is a far, far better thing that I do now than I have... And other ridiculous stuff like that.

The revolutionaries were a wonderfully egalitarian people who loved and hated impartially. They loved capital punishment and hated aristocrats in equal measure.

Even clever people like Charles Dickens were fooled by the language, which was surprising because Dickens wasn't born until years after the rebels had run out of aristocrats. You would think that this and being English would have made him an expert on the French revolution.

As it turned out he was even wrong about the title of his story "A Tale Of Two Cities." It was really "A Sale's On At Kitty's" - the bakery where they sold long crusty bread.

Anyway, it all turned out well because the French have now learned to speak English – as they should have done in the first place. But they have never quite reconciled themselves to this ignominy.

Eating out in France can be a trying experience – especially for kids who have become accustomed to slurping and burping at Carl's junior. And being forced to eat with a knife and fork without taking lessons is no fun either.

French waiters will say stuff like, "If the food gets all over your face you don't belong in this place" or "If your food gets all over this place I'll get in your face, and other unreasonable variations on that theme.

But here is a bit of information that might be useful. French waiters are only able to speak English if you speak to them in fluent French. Then they will not understand a word you are saying. But if you speak English they will only speak fluent French.

This will explain why French restaurants add 15% gratuity to the bill. They are not likely to get rich on tips if they rely on the goodwill of happy, satisfied patrons. So they don't.

In France, a special commission is now struggling to restore the original French language to its former glory. It's been many years since Al Gore invented the Internet but the French have just discovered that English seems to have become its primary language.

They are right to be upset. I mean why did Bill Gates use English terminology in his programs when he knows very well that French is the primary language of America?

Understandably, the French can't abide any kind of national arrogance. As everyone knows, they hold the world copyright on all varieties of this presumption of superiority and should have been consulted.

But we should concede that some suggested French language reforms for the Internet make a lot of sense. For a start they don't like us using "@" because "@" means "at", which is an English word. They suggest that it should be called "arobase or "arrobe." But we may still use "@" for "at" if it's called something French. Americans might call it something else.

It's interesting that, a few years ago, the French commission, which is advocating these sensible changes, suggested that Internet start-up companies should be called "young sprouts," which, in French is "jeunes pousses." Well, who are they trying to fool? Everyone knows that "jeunes pousses" means "yellow cats".

So until Bill Gates and Al Gore learn the new language I think it would be a far, far better thing if they stay away from France - even if they hear there's a sale on a kitty's.

32. WINE WAITER IN YOUR CELLAR

Now is the time for you to become acquainted with the mysteries of wine slurping. Don't wait for party time to become privy to those carefully guarded secrets of the somewhat snobby society of sommeliers.

Well, you're lucky because I've just spent all of twenty arduous minutes studying a connoisseur's manual of fine wines. So it's my duty to give both of you the benefit of this vast albeit newly acquired knowledge.

Okay, my advice is never mind the wine; concentrate on the rules of etiquette that must be followed if you are ever to become a successful wine snob.

To best display your knowledge of the secret protocols necessary to membership in the ancient craft it is advisable to employ a wine waiter for the evening. This will miraculously improve the quality of your wine.

But you should ensure that he stays out of sight until called for. The dignified effect that you seek will be destroyed if he is seen staggering around the dining room helping himself to the countess' fries.

It's best to keep him in the cellar with your 6 bottles of Outer Mongolian red, where he can practice how to keep the labels covered with his hand while pouring the stuff.

Yes, we all know that sniffing the cork is a sure sign of wine wisdom but nobody knows why. This makes it easier.

All you do is slowly wave the proffered cork under your nose and ooh and aah and give an enigmatic little smile. Your guests will gnash their teeth in admiration hoping that you've burned the turkey.

But like most things it's not quite as simple as it sounds. To avoid a bloodbath it's imperative that you remember a very important rule about cork sniffing. Sharp edged screw tops should not be sniffed. Under no circumstances should they be waved under the nose – unless one of your guests is a plastic surgeon.

Latour is a very famous French wine. At a recent tasting the wine was priced at $1,300 a bottle. No not a barrel, just one of those little bottles for two. To those of us who have been drinking last Tuesday's vintage at $3.95 a gallon this may seem a lot to pay for a smelly cork.

But even the experts are sometimes confused. At this tasting, some thought the $1,300 bottle of Latour tasted like dill pickles. Naturally, if I had made this wine I would have said that this was exactly the flavor I had been aiming for. I too would have kept quiet about dropping my deli sandwich into the barrel.

Another expert said the wine had a "stewed tomato aroma". And some thought it safer just to wax poetic. It was "like a spiritual experience." It was "supple and silky", "voluptuous and velvety", or "sippingly mouth drying" and stuff.

For wines to be enjoyed at peak flavor, color and bouquet, they must be stored in a climate that recreates the conditions of a natural belowground wine cellar without mildew. They should be maintained at a natural 70-degree humidity. Our family room, when I was a kid, would have been ideal if it had not been for all that mildew on the cat and granddads beard.

If you are determined to be the only wine expert at your party, you must personally greet every guest at the front door. You should ask if they know anything about cork sniffing. If they look baffled you hug them and push them into the dining room. If they say "Oh, yes, I'm an expert cork sniffer, you push them down the steps and as they sprawl in the street you shout sweetly, "sorry, you must have the wrong house, Merry Christmas," or whatever the occasion might be.

It has been shown that red wine can prevent heart attacks. So if you drink ten or twelve bottles a day it will help your heart to withstand the trauma of all those liver transplants you're going to need.

Finally, although it's rare nowadays, grapes were once crushed under foot. Experts say it definitely affects the smell of the cork. So remember; never drink wine in a restaurant where the waiter has purple feet.

33. A LA CARTE

What I want to know is, why is it that now people are eating out more often, shopping carts getting bigger? It doesn't make sense. If we eat out more often it means we eat in less often. So it should be the restaurants that get bigger not the shopping carts.

People are definitely getting bigger too. This is because when eating out we invariably order all the tasty, succulent, delicious, greasy, unhealthy stuff. Then we blame the restaurant. It took us by surprise so it's not our fault. We were just sitting there thinking of salad and a waiter came along and shoved unhealthy food down our throats.

The trick is to plan what you are going to order before leaving home. After a hard day's work you should say to your partner: "Tell you what my dear: Let's go out for a nice, fresh lettuce leaf tonight."

But before you get too excited at the prospect I should warn you that you won't get many takers unless you promise raw carrots and celery for dessert.

In a way, eating at a restaurant is the same as shopping at a supermarket. Either way the food is to go. So after we've eaten out and become real big and paid the real big check, we could be trundled out to the parking lot in a real big shopping cart and stacked in our car. Care would be taken to stack us upright so that food doesn't spill out and roll all over the floor.

This way you get to take your shopping home in the usual way but are spared the agony of choosing whether it will be carried in plastic or paper because you yourself will be the bag. And, you'll never again have to hear, "What's for dinner?" because you are already wrapped around it.

I wonder why nobody has thought of this before. Of course you would need to order "A La Carte" if you want to be wheeled to your car.

I'm sure you know how I hate to say, "When I was young," but when you are old you can't help it because that's what you were before you got old. Anyway when I was young there were no supermarkets, and the local Mom and Pop store didn't even supply shopping bags let alone shopping carts. We would take the baby's hat to the store for our groceries. It didn't need wheels because the food was small and could easily have been eaten right there in the store.

Unfortunately, unlike shopping in today's supermarkets, you couldn't eat your dinner in the aisles before you actually got to the checkout. So this is probably one reason why people were poorer.

The problem was that everything was out of reach behind the counter. Nothing was pre-packaged and you had to ask for what you wanted. Then the clerk would rummage around on the shelves behind him, cut a chunk of whatever you had ordered and wrap it in newspaper.

But I should point out that he didn't wrap it in newspaper out of concern for your hygiene. After all, the food had lain unwrapped on the shelf under a load of other junk for months so there was no point in suddenly trying to keep it clean.

You see we never ate enough food to make it worthwhile for the germs to colonize it. So the poor little bugs just hung around waiting for penicillin to be invented so they could end it all. Yes it's true there was one small glitch in our system of hygiene called bubonic plague but that didn't last very long.

In those days shopping carts were used for transporting bits and pieces around the neighborhood but never used to carry shopping. You will have noticed that some die-hard traditionalists still stick to those quaint old ways.

Anyway, on the weekend, dad would bundle the family into the family shopping cart and run us down to the sea. No he didn't do this so he could drown us all with one quick push, but if you had met our family you would understand how tempting that could be.

You can bet that one day when SUVs get bigger they will be used as shopping carts, and sixteen wheelers will be polished for a run to the sea. No one, however wise, can stop the march of regress.

Meanwhile, shopping carts are getting bigger. Maybe it's just optimism on the part of the supermarkets. Perhaps the only people who actually fill the things to the top are the ones who lie in wait at the checkout stand so they can push in front of me and my tube of toothpaste.

And judging by my own experience they usually pay with bundles of coupons and ten dollars in pennies to make up the difference. Still, I must admit that this only happens when I'm in a hurry - It's probably covered by the same law that dictates all the lights will turn green as you reach them, but only if you are early for an appointment.

So I decided to shop online and took the trouble to squeeze an enormous shopping cart next to my computer. But the service is very slow. I've been shopping for two weeks now and so far nobody has put any food in the thing. Perhaps we should just go out for a lettuce leaf.

34. PAINT THE CEILING

Today we take for granted such things as equality, political correctness and eating every day. But when I was a kid people were created unequal. Men, for instance, had it all their own way. Every day they went to work in the mines for a measly 14 hours, seven days a week, while their wives stayed home in the kitchen cooking, scrubbing clothes and looking after the 15 kids.

There were fewer divorces, of course. This was because it wouldn't have made much difference. I mean they never saw each other anyway. And even if the brutal husband had looked forward all day to beating his wife, he was too tired when he got home so he would give her a cuddle instead. Then he would soon be coming home to 16 kids instead of fifteen. And so it went.

A really caring man would occasionally ask his wife how many kids he had and would she write down their names and ages - and a brief description so he would recognize them if he met one in the pub.

Guys are definitely better people than they once were. But they seem to be, what can I say, a little diminished? I mean when they worked 14 hours in the mines, they had 15 kids but now with a whole weekend off, they have 2.5.

Can it be that leisure and equality are less productive than labor and chauvinism? Was it Darwin who said that every action causes an opposite and equal reaction?

Famous artists of old, much loved by today's women for their sensitivity, would now be viewed with a more jaundiced eye.

As long ago as the 15th century, there were men who tried really hard to be equal, but it's not easy to do when you are Leonardo da Vinci or Michelangelo. Neither one of them ever offered to help with the dishes or changed a diaper. They figured they'd just go ahead and achieve great things and hope no one got mad.

They had no idea how to be sensitive or cry at sad murals. But now there are ways to make insensitive men cry. "You can be a genius after you finish doing the dishes and diapers," is a one of them.

Can you imagine Michelangelo today, taking 5 years to paint a ceiling?

Mrs. Michelangelo: "Hey, Mike, you've been up there on your back for 5 years. What the heck are you doing?"

Michelangelo: "I'm painting the ceiling, dear."

Mrs. M: "Oh, yeah, well, when are you going to paint our fence?"

Mr. M: "This is the high renaissance period, dear; I'll do the fence when I come down."

Mrs. M: "Yeah, right. Like you'd do a job where you had to stand up. Why don't you just get a longer brush, Eh? And get that statue of David out of the yard; it's frightening the dog."

Today that ceiling would be known as the - "he promised to come back and finish this after dinner but painted his fence instead" - ceiling. Fences would soon be famous.

Visitors would stare in awe at the brushwork. People would take their own fences to Antiques Road Shows for appraisal. And Tom Sawyer, that sly little future Enron executive would never have sub contracted his fence out for an apple core.

Not too many people know this but that famous picture by Leonardo da Vinci, called Mona Lisa, was of his wife Gertrude, laughing uproariously at a hilarious Tuscan joke.

Her expression was meant to show how deliriously happy women were in those days. Well, she did her best.

Okay, Leonardo was a darned chauvinist pig but it's hard to be pleasant when you've just invented helicopters and no one will invent engines for 300 years.

You can bet that today, if Van Gough cut off his ear, his wife would soon complain about having to pick up his pencil every time he forgot there was nothing to put it behind.

Vincent was born when men were still rotten but he wasn't totally insensitive. You see, when his wife complained that he never listened to her, he gave her his ear so he could hear what she said even when he was out on his 12-hour shift. Okay, I guess we men are still a little insensitive. But I always cry a lot when I have to do the dishes. Does that count?

35. A CASE FOR PAWOBS

Last week we discussed the merits of running ten miles early every morning for twenty years to win a gold medal. You will be happy to know that we are not going to do that anymore. Today we are going to discuss "Pawobs." You have probably been a "Pawob" yourself at some time. Perhaps, you still are.

If this is the case, don't be ashamed because there are thousands of you. I have even been one myself. Quite recently.

"Pawobs" is what the Airlines call passengers without bags. When they lose your bag they have this friendly habit of adding insult to injury by calling you names. Pawob is just one of them.

ME: "Excuse me miss, I don't like to interrupt just when you're nodding off but I seem to have lost my bags."

AIRLINE PERSON: "Oh, so you're a Pawob then, aren't you?"

ME: "Well, I don't think so miss. In fact I've never even been to India."

AIRLINE PERSON: Oh, really, you should try it sometime. It's lovely this time of year. That's probably where your bags are.

ME: "But I booked to London."

AIRLINE PERSON: "Then why on earth did you send your bags to India?"

ME: "But I didn't, I sent them to London."

AIRLINE PERSON: (patting my head kindly and giving me a lump of sugar) Then how did you expect them to get to India, Mr.Cycle?

ME: My name's not Cycle it's Cicale.

AIRLINE PERSON: "Ah, there you are then, if your name were Cycle your bags would be in Chicago by now waiting for you to arrive at the carousel. Next time get your name right, okay,"

ME: (Becoming a little dizzy and blinking rapidly.) "But my name is ... But I booked to ..."

And so it goes. The good news is that if your bags are completely lost, some Airlines will award you up to $2,500. But this is not based on what you paid for the lost contents but on the depreciated value of those contents.

This means that I should be able to claim $2,500 for the loss of my valuable wardrobe. But if they were unkind enough to calculate the true value of my best suit, two ties, one shoe and three socks, it would come to about $3.50.

In case you are wondering about my shirt, I usually wear it to travel. This means that I will, at least get to keep it on my back until I get the bill for dinner and a cup of coffee in England, then it too will be gone.

Naturally, if there were no depreciation rule and we could automatically get $2,500, the Taj Mahal would be full of $2,500 lost bags containing one suit and three socks.

US: "Er miss, I've lost my bag. I think you must have sent it to India, so where's my $2,500? (Try not to chuckle behind your hand, it makes them suspicious.)

THEM: "Okay, Mr. Pawob, what makes you think it went to India.

US: "Well, that's easy miss, I labeled it for London; where else could it have gone?"

THEM: "How about Chicago Mr. Cycle?"

Okay, nobody said it would be easy to get $2,500 for a $3.00 suit and three socks.

But, enough with the negativity. If you are one of the approximately 500,000 people whose bags go missing permanently, all you need to do is submit a proper claim. Once you have done this you will be sent another more detailed form.

Those of us who are cynical enough to see where this is going will usually give up their claim right there.

Anyway, at this point you are warned that if you fail to complete this second form your claim could be delayed. You are not expected to notice that you are already being delayed by the second form.

The Airline will then refer your claim to the central office and negotiations between you and the airline will begin. So you see, we are still just at the beginning.

But how about this: Sometimes the airline will offer you free tickets on future flights. If you take them up on this don't take any bags - or if you do take bags don't label them for London unless you are going to India. Also hang on very tightly to your carry on bag, especially if it has your correct name and address on it. That kind of carelessness could cause the thing to disappear completely.

But everything has a positive side. Even in adversity there is opportunity. If you are a criminal on the run from the police - or from the Mafia for that matter - go to an airline and have yourself labeled as cargo for London. No one will ever find you again. But, of course, don't try to claim the $2,500 for the loss of yourself – especially if you've depreciated a lot. Also, it would help to learn conversational Urdu.

36. GENERATION GAP

The generation gap wasn't always as wide as it is today. Of course, there were always young people and middle-aged people; but really old people of forty-two were a rarity. And they never told kids about the good old days because they couldn't remember having any. Also, there was no point in trying to impress kids with tales of walking to school through 20-foot snowdrifts when everyone was still doing it.

For hundreds of years things didn't really change much. They kind of oozed along slowly. Music gradually increased in volume from a whisper to a sigh to a hum. It stayed right there until someone had the bright idea of calling kids between 13 and 19, teenagers instead of kids.

Well this turned out to be more than just the bestowal of a new designation. Its recipients underwent a racial and cultural metamorphosis. It may be hard to believe but for countless generations, before teenagers were invented, parents and kids spoke the same language.

In those far off days, only adults were privy to the intricacies of modern technological advances – stuff like people-propelled-ploughs and labor-intensive-water pumps.

Unlike today's fledgling computer experts, 12-year-olds were not yet advanced enough to teach adults how to uninstall a blocked sewage pipe, or edit the drainage ditch behind the outhouse - or, perhaps they were too considerate to show they could do it better. I guess if today's technology were still all about hard labor and muck, kids would probably bow to our superior knowledge and admit that it was too advanced for them to handle.

Years ago there was no point in adult entrepreneurs producing amusing, time wasting, fun stuff when kids didn't yet have the power to force their parents to buy it for them. And even if kids could have come up with the power, they would have to come up with the money too, because adults didn't have any.

Of course, adults were still in charge – which is why the world was in such a mess for hundreds of years.

We can only hope that, due to their superior education and greater autonomy, kids will make a mess much faster than we ever could. That's what progress is all about. We want our kids to have more than we had – even if it's just more of a mess.

If it were not for this evolutionary system, the darned old world would be floundering in the mire endlessly, on and on and on, forever boomboxless and teeming with Crosbys and Sinatras. Is that scary or what?

Naturally, we old time kids were just as high-spirited as today's kids. But before being given the magical honorific of "teenager" we were not so overtly rebellious.

Nothing is so stimulating or likely to spur rebellion as belonging to a privileged and honored peer group. Yes, you might think that being privileged and honored would produce the opposite effect, since it doesn't leave too much to be rebellious about. But this only works if you employ pure logic without considering the influence of human nature, and now I'm getting a headache.

Anyway, even without a peer support group, kids have always been somewhat mischievous and wayward. When Shakespeare put on the first performance of Romeo and Juliet, not one kid came forward and took responsibility for changing the fake poison for cyanide.

But, you see, it was more an act of compassion than mischief. In those days life was tough for actors. There were always replacement Romeos and Juliets waiting in the wings to drink the cyanide. Well, when you haven't had a gig for 5 years, a one-night stand is better than nothing – especially when your amazingly realistic death scene is sure to be a huge success with the critics.

The language has certainly changed since Shakespeare's time. You must have noticed how kids love the question mark. Almost every sentence ends with an upward inflection:

"So this dude comes up to me, you know? And he goes, yo? And I goes back, like, yo dude?" Just imagine, "To be or not to be, dude? That is the question, dude?" It loses something.

Well, I think the reason for the question mark is that it leaves every sentence open to interpretation. You can decide it means whatever suits your mood at the time. It's certainly non-confrontational for people to hear what they want to hear. Adults don't understand this. They are sooo uncool?

But every cloud has a silver lining, right? One day our teenagers will have teenagers of their own – and we get to watch? How cool is that dude?

37. HUMANE DINNER

Over in the Blue Ridge Mountains of Virginia there is an English style pub where the sound of happy, doomed animals wafts across the parking lot and into the dining room.

Everywhere joyful gobbles and clucks can be heard vying with cheerful oinks and merry moos. This is an animal resort, you see. A last resort, as it happens.

The playful animals rib each other about who will achieve the best pan tan. "And my dear," cries a happy chicken, "Did you know the new barbeque is air conditioned?"

These fortunate animals are destined to become the happiest shepherd's pie and spare ribs in the land. Very good, but wait.

As far as we know, vegetation is the only life form that can exist without consuming other life forms. It doesn't hunt or gather, maim or kill; it just sits and sucks from the Earth and from the sun. Vegetation is, in fact, at the bottom of the food chain – unless you want to include the earth itself.

And just because vegetables don't scream when hacked with a knife they are considered fair game. No sound - no pain - no guilt. If vegetation could moo or cluck or oink, some people would starve – or rationalize.

You would think that, by now, fish would have learned to scream, or something. I mean, who would regard fishing as the sport of benign old men or as a hobby for dads to teach their kids, if fish bellowed in pain?

Imagine the fuss a pig would make. "Hey, come on Joe, pull out the hook and throw the critter back in the hog-pen so someone else can have a go." I don't think this would catch on.

The Hunter's Inn Tavern, animal resort is an English-style pub in Virginia which has become the first U.S. restaurant to get an animal welfare group's stamp of approval for the humane treatment of animals on its menu. "The groups certification offers assurance that the meat or poultry on a plate was not raised in inhumane conditions," said Adele Douglass, of Humane Farm Animal Care.

Well, it's clear that animals raised humanely don't mind becoming dinner. But to make it clearer they should stop the little critters from screaming.

It's a good thing that lettuce and apples are pain free – we think – maybe. I'll bet it would keep the doctor away – and everyone else too - if an apple screamed every time you took a bite. Self-righteous people would declare, "Oh, I don't eat apples, you know, but you go ahead – if you must."

But even under humane conditions animals still make a noise when becoming dinner. Such ingratitude. And you can't shove a gag in a pig's mouth because, to a pig, everything is dinner. It doesn't care if the gag screams, down it goes. Anyway it's not nice to slaughter something at dinnertime – except maybe a telemarketer.

Naturally, we prefer to be slaughtered than be tele-marketed, but a pig doesn't get that choice. In fact a pig might actually enjoy talking on the phone to a kindred spirit at dinnertime.

The Hunter's Inn tavern is owned by Sandy Lerner, who said, "We want to introduce people to looking at food in a new way." Okay, how do you look at your food? Do you frown at it? Well, sandy wants you to stop. Give it a smile, or something, I guess.

Sandy also raises humane veal. But veal on your plate must be approached differently. When you smile, include a little baby talk, maybe a gurgle or two. Veal just loves that.

Years ago my dad was an unsung early pioneer of the humane treatment principle. He would insist we treat our animals kindly. He was all heart, you see. He explained that when we needed to slaughter one of them it would come running trustingly to the sound of daddy's voice – even if daddy were carrying an axe. For the uninitiated, an axe is an old fashioned anti scream device. Still none of us was allowed to frown at our dinner – except my dad, if there wasn't enough of it.

Evidently, PETA has been urging Kentucky Fried Chicken to adopt more humane standards. But this is unfair, I mean, is there any painless way to remove a chicken's nuggets?

And, you can be sure that if lettuce had their nuggets removed before slaughter, there would be no outcry at all – and certainly not from the lettuce, because... But, we've already been there, right?

38. INTERMEDIARY DINNER

Is it ironic, or what? I mean, we're told that to enjoy a longer life we have to suffer. So is the operative word here, "enjoy," or "suffer?" Only a masochist could do both at the same time, right?

Well, according to cardiologists and dieticians and other killjoys, you can only become immortal if you eat grassy stuff and exercise 10 times a day. Okay, that's the suffering bit, where's the enjoy bit.

In the old days if you made people eat grassy stuff and exercise 10 times a day they would kill themselves. Immortality would be a threat not a promise. I mean, who wants to eat grass for a hundred years? It would be hard enough just making it to twenty five.

Okay, you're right, you are what you eat. So, let's compromise. What's wrong with eating something that eats the grass first so that it becomes the kind of grass we can eat and actually enjoy? What's wrong with having an intermediary – like a cow?

Not too long ago people crammed steaks and pints of double cream and French fries cooked in pans that were so inundated with animal fats they mooed at you. In a restaurant they said stuff like: "Now are you sure this meat is deliciously unhealthy?" and "are these eggs guaranteed high cholesterol and tasty?" Okay, they died at 23 but always with a smile on their face.

Living longer has become an end in itself. Whoever lives longest is the winner. It doesn't have to be fun. But what good is a touchdown dance when you're the only one left in the field, eating grass? And then you die anyway – just like the loser – who was, at least, smiling.

If murderers were sentenced to a hundred years of eating grass and exercising every day, Liberals would make noises about cruel and unusual stuff. They would scream for a more humanitarian punishment - like the death penalty.

And then we are told to keep our weight down by eating nothing but whole grains, vegetables and fiber. But, for heaven's sake, that's what they give chickens to fatten them up, isn't it? I mean why don't they give them steaks and ice cream to fatten them up? It works for us, right?

Now there is even a report urging women to take more care of their bodies. It seems that, "in the U.S., pregnancy is associated with an average of five to six pounds of weight gain."

Okay, somebody tell me how you can avoid putting on five or six pounds when you've just added eight pounds of baby? It's the kind of accuracy-challenged rationale the CIA would use to liberate people from their dinner.

Now in case you're wondering, I didn't jump to these conclusions without checking them out first. I ate six doughnuts and went to join the rest of the human race at the health club.

Well, after taking a long, thoughtful stroll around my body, the instructor was very encouraging. He said that a stroll around my body could be used to show new members the sickening things neglect can do to an already repulsive structure. He suggested that in my present state of health there were two ways I could go. (I didn't care too much for his phraseology.)

He said we could start with something easy like raising and lowering my eyelids ten times every minute. Or I could play tennis doubles for an hour with three ex Wimbledon champions. He assured me that they could get me from the tennis court to the intensive care unit in fifteen minutes. They did it all the time. This was very reassuring.

We started with the eyelids. But all that seeing and not seeing and then seeing again made me dizzy. After a few sessions my eyes developed a kind of unfocussed glaze and my eyebrows were permanently raised. The instructor said I looked surprised and horrified at the same time. "This doesn't usually happen until people see their bill," he said, thoughtfully.

133

Perhaps I take after my grandfather who hated exercise. Oh, he liked to eat. He had no aversion to moving his jaws up and down and would do it at every opportunity. He could probably have been a gold medalist if there had been a food-chewing event.

But predictably, he paid for his unhealthy lifestyle when he was only 35. Yes, my grandmother died of a cholesterol and fat deficiency from too much walking to the health food store, so he had to get his own dinner for the next 70 years. Serves him right. Okay, has anyone seen my doughnuts?

39. DID NEANDERTHALS NEED HELP?

Let's face it; civilization is not all it's cracked up to be. It's unnatural. And it involves so much work. It inflicts all kinds of indignities and pains that are avoided by lesser beings. And it starts as soon as we are born.

I mean, how many primitive beings slap a baby just for being born? None. But a welcome to our world, beating of civilized babies is mandatory. And it's often administered by a doctor and doesn't stop until the little guy cries. This gives the kid confidence that his doctor will always be able to stop his pain. Of course, he will still cry when he gets the bill. The doctor won't be able to stop that.

Monkeys are not civilized. This is why a mother monkey won't allow anyone to beat up her kid as soon as it's born? She's primitive. This is why, instead of a beating she licks it gently for a while and if it cries she feeds it or swings it through the trees until it stops.

Okay, it's not civilization per se that's bad. Social order is good. It won't be easy, but we should try to hang on to it a while longer if we can. The point is that now we've gone over the top. Why can't we have social order without all the troublesome trappings?

Being a monkey or a lion or even a dog or cat is so easy. You wake up in the morning and you scratch and yawn and if you like, you go back to sleep. Why is that so bad? Why can't we all do it? What great cosmic catastrophe would we spawn by scratching and going back to sleep?

No primitive being ever wakes from sleep crying out desperately, "oh, no, oh my gosh, not another day, not already." Sometimes followed by "Help me, help me, help me." Can you imagine your cat doing that? Of course not. Only civilized beings do that. It shows how smart we are.

Our first civilized duty on waking is to take a shower. No one knows exactly why. How did it start? We can't be dirty already. We showered yesterday. Not so very long ago we would simply wash in a basin of water every Friday night. That's why they are known as the good old days.

In those days, instead of taking a shower, you could lie in bed ten minutes longer and scratch and maybe smile a little. Well, it was our civilized duty to stop all that nonsense wasn't it?

Did you know that Neanderthals had bigger brains than we have? That's puzzling, isn't it? But it was probably because they spent more time using them introspectively instead of feeding them on a diet of entertainment and gadgets and constant artificial external stimulation. It was probably all this stuff that made our brains shrink.

Think how far we've come from the caves. Just look around at the gadgets and the furniture and carpets. You can only afford it all because you spend most of your time elsewhere – operating someone else's gadgets.

And what about that beautiful, comfortable king size bed? A Neanderthal only had straw on the floor of a cave but he spent considerably more time lying on it than you do on your king size And never once did anyone tell him to clean the garage or mow the field. This is why he never woke up saying

"Oh my gosh, help me, help me, help me." Why would he say, "help me?" He didn't need any help to yawn and scratch and go back to sleep.

Certainly, it's true that before we were civilized we had to compete for a place by the fire. We killed each other, sometimes for no valid reason and hoarded food and stole each other's mates and didn't use deodorant. But now, thank goodness, things are different. Now we use deodorant.

Okay, that's enough introspection for today; it's giving me a headache; now where's that remote?

40. PARENTS TO BLAME
FOR FAULTY FACULTIES

If you think all that stuff about the weaker sex and the stronger sex is nonsense you are mistaken. You see, this somewhat sexist notion has now been proved valid by Sebastian Kraemer, consultant psychiatrist at the Tavistock and Portman National Health Service Trust in England.

He has shown conclusively that women are indeed stronger than men. This will clear up a mystery that has plagued women for centuries. Why, if men are so tough, don't they have the babies? So, now we know, don't we?

Kraemer's research showed that the male fetus is at greater risk of death or damage, and by the time the baby is born, a boy is four to six weeks less developed than a girl.

But does this mean that when boys are first exposed to light, they develop in a more negative way? Perhaps this is what the princess meant by "some day my prints will come."

And, it seems, that males are more vulnerable than females from the moment they are conceived, and parents should treat them more sensitively than they do. According to Kraemer, the fact that boys are treated as more resilient than their sisters means that they suppress some faculties.

"There is a social pressure not to let boys be too weak and to toughen them up." Kraemer said. "A boy who is full of sensitivity and vulnerability will have shut down a lot of these faculties within the first two years."

So, okay, perhaps, deep down, men really are very loving and sensitive, but because of parental suppression these faculties are channeled in new and strange directions. Take Mike Tyson, for instance. He was only dancing around with someone he liked a lot and if his sensitivity had been left alone he might have just lovingly nibbled his partner's ear.

But the theory is still a bit shaky. I mean, it's not consistent because there was nothing wrong with his partner's vulnerability and sensitivity was there? He wasn't afraid to shed a tear or two, was he? No, he was only afraid that Mike might ask him to dance again.

But, I guess now we know that Tyson was not being a macho brute but just showing his feminine side - which is stronger - instead of... Well, it's complicated, and now I'm getting a headache again.

But I'm quite sure that most men will not mind being the weaker sex from now on. If their parents don't suppress them they will be able to watch sad movies without taking quick swipes at their eyes and sniffing a lot as though they think it's all silly nonsense.

Now big, hairy men will be able to sniffle and say, "Oh, how lovely. Why can't you women be sensitive and wonderful like Tom Hanks? And when are you going to go to the Empire State Building and not find me there and get sad and look for me and stuff?"

And women will watch football on TV with the girls and drink beer and make rude noises and blame it all on the dog. Naturally, if it's a sensitive, male dog he will be very hurt and cry a little.

And to augment the theory, it has now been discovered that men are too sensitive to watch soccer without putting themselves at risk of sudden death. You see, up until now they have forced themselves to watch this blood sport because they were suppressed into believing they were strong enough to take it.

Now, scientists in the Netherlands have found that "50 percent more men died from heart attack or stroke on the day of their countries dramatic exit from the 1996 European championship than on an ordinary day."

And then, significantly, it goes on to say, "No corresponding increase occurred in women." Well, that's because they're stronger - and maybe because they didn't watch the game since they had been taught they were sensitive and vulnerable.

To make sure it wasn't a seasonal rise, Diederick Grobbee, professor at the University Medical Center in Utrecht, also compared the deaths with the same period in 1995 and 1997.

"What happened was that one game in particular showed a particular increase in fatalities, and that was the quarter-final," said Grobbee.

"It was a dramatic match," he said, panting heavily and clutching his chest. "It was nil-nil," he screamed, and was decided by penalties," "France won the shoot out 5-4 after Clarence Seedorf saw his spot kick saved and France kept a hundred percent record. The crowd went wild – goaaaalll!" He broke down, sobbing.

You will probably notice how well Professor Grobbee managed to suppress his sensitive side and allow himself to get carried away and forget all about men dying of stroke and heart attacks and, enthusiastically, describe in great detail, the game that caused all the carnage. This was his parents' fault because they suppressed his faculties.

But if we are going to accept the validity of this theory, that women are the stronger sex, we should have a reversal of men's traditional role as chair puller-outer and door opener for the weaker sex. My wife says she doesn't mind opening the door for me when I take out the garbage, but she's hanging on to my razor until I promise not to shave my legs again. Women can be so insensitive.

41. WE HAVE WAYS OF MAKING YOU TALK

These days to get ahead it is essential to be a good public speaker. No, that does not mean that you will need to be well behaved it just means you have to talk good and proper. Anyone who has given a speech at a marine barracks or convocation of coal miners will know that it's quite easy.

But to speak at a meeting of the local temperance society takes more skill. This is not because the miners and marines are dumb, quite the opposite. It's because the temperance group is, for the most part, sober. And to make matters worse you will be expected to follow their example.

Also you will be required to make sense, which is not a problem when speaking to the marines or the coal miners, who won't care either way. Okay, then, let us proceed on the assumption that your audience is sober.

In public speaking it's important to know what it is you are trying to say. An extemporaneous speaker can work directly from a simple outline.

Well, for a start don't use the word extemporaneous. It will only confuse the audience and they will miss the rest of your speech while trying to work out what it means. I'm confused myself and I just used it.

It's all right to use humor. But it's important that the type of humor is suitable for the occasion. At a wedding you should not say, "Though I walk through the valley of the shadow of death." People will begin to doubt the success of your own marriage.

It's true that some people would rather die than make a public speech. When asked to speak at a funeral, these people would obviously be happier in the box than on the pulpit? So in the end it's all a matter of choice.

The skill required to make a good speech will vary depending on the location. Sometimes you will use fewer words and more body language. You must have heard of the Italian who asked his grandson how the telephone worked. "Why, you just pick up that thing with your left hand and dial with your right," said the lad.

"Both hands? Exclaimed the grandfather. You need both hands to work this machine? Then how do you talk?"

It will help you if you study other speakers. You can learn a lot from their style of delivery. When a speaker is unable to speak unless continually interrupted mid sentence by someone in the audience, the speaker is obviously married. These are tricks you will learn as you go along.

The ability to act is another essential of speechmaking. Some of the best acting is done by stars congratulating other stars who have just won an Oscar. If you are going to be insincere for heavens sake make it convincing – especially if you plan to be a politician.

To keep the attention of your audience, one of the most important rules is to make your meaning clear.

At a convention of businessmen a speaker was heard to say, "Business is what – when you don't have any – you go out of." And just because I can't think of a better way to say it doesn't mean it's all right. Of course same of you might say, "That is the sort of English up with which I will not put." Well, not me neither.

Yes, if you think about it for ten minutes you get the meaning. But in that time your audience could get up and leave. Of course if you are one of those speakers who keep being interrupted by the audience, you won't care.

Naturally, I have not always been an expert public speaker. At one time I used to go on too long. So at one of my speeches the chairman was given a gavel and a board to strike so that I would know when to stop.

Well I didn't hear the warning and when the chairman made to strike the board for the third time he accidentally struck the guy in the next chair on the head. The chairman cried out, "Are you all right?" And, as his semi conscious partner slid under the table he answered, "no, hit me again, I can still hear him." I tried to get at the mallet so I could oblige but I was restrained.

42. WAKE UP CALL

Sometimes, modern methods of preventing us from shuffling of this mortal coil can be inconvenient. So, there you are, sick and old and lying peacefully in your own bed, dreaming of better days, when the ambulance crew pounces. "How do you feel, how do you feel, lie still, don't talk, answer me."

Well, you don't know it yet but being sick and lying peacefully in your own bed will soon be added to the better days you were dreaming of.

You have probably noticed that hospital is no place for a sick person. Only really fit Olympic athletes should be allowed to stay in a hospital overnight. This is because they are more likely to survive the noise of cheering crowds and loud voices on ten minutes sleep a night.

Of course it's true that most staff members are concerned for your welfare. They try to keep a constant eye on you. That's why they switch on the overhead searchlight to see if you're sleeping peacefully. It's for your own good.

This method helps ensure that they will notice if you somehow, manage to drop off for ten minutes, which is always just before you hear, "wake up, dear, wake up, breakfast will be here in forty five minutes."

Strangely enough, this is the best time to grab a little sleep. You see, the night crew is being debriefed and the morning crew is not due to take over yet. For a few minutes it's almost as good as being at death's door in your own bed at home.

Yes, it's probably true that, had you stayed home you might have shuffled off this mortal coil by now, but when you are being jabbed with needles to put stuff in or take stuff out or made to use the bedpan or wash without rinsing while in a sleep-deprived daze, death's door doesn't seem so bad anymore.

I guess France in August is the best place and time for a hospital stay. This is because everyone in France is on vacation through August. All the medical professionals draw straws and three unlucky nurses and one doctor are made to take care of five million patients.

Naturally, they are not heartless. The doctor can be reached by cell phone at a hotel in Tahiti. If he is called he will rush right back and arrive exactly at 10am on September 1st.

Incidentally, that's when the nurses come back to help take care of the survivors who are often suffering from "too much sleeping peacefully with no noise syndrome".

You must have seen the long French loaf of bread called a baguette. Well it was designed so that French patients could sleep with their breakfast and not be disturbed by wake up calls. Their breakfast is stretched out lazily right there in bed beside them. I mean that's why it's called a loaf, right? After taking a long loaf you take a long loaf, I guess.

The x-ray room is a fun place for old sick people. You lie on a metal shelf and are told to keep perfectly still with your arm or leg twisted at a grotesque angle. If this were done to prisoners in Iraq there would be an international outcry.

And the funny thing is that you are there because you can't twist you arm or leg at a grotesque angle.

Then you are told not to move, not to breathe and not to blink. Well to an old person, lying on a slab not moving or breathing or blinking is disturbingly like a dry run – especially when they bring in students so that they will recognize the real thing when they see it.

But to be fair, you can't blame young people for being jealous of old age. It has many compensations. You only get to do it once and even if you make a mess of it, who cares? It's not as though it's going to ruin your career, is it? No one's going to say, "you made a mess of that, you're fired from old age," are they?

Also, when you are young they never put you on a treadmill and tell you to run for your life; but if you're old and survive fifteen minutes on this contraption and regain consciousness in less then an hour you are regarded as fit enough to give back all your social security payments for medication. They even give you a bunch of prescriptions to help you do it.

On top of all this you are expected to socialize with other old people who only want to complain about being made to lie still and hold their breath and have grotesque angled arms and legs. I'm glad I'm not like that.

Of course many of us have now been helped to reach the age we said we didn't want to live to be. But, we said it before we knew there would be a dance next Saturday
at the Stardust ballroom.

It's wonderful. We never have any of those silly dances where you tap someone on the shoulder to take their partner. We just wait until someone collapses, and jump right in. Anyway, while I'm waiting, I'd like to show you this weird x-ray of my ...

43. LEMON AID

My very first car was a used Ford advertised in the local paper by John Smith. As soon as he answered the phone it was obvious he loved that car so much that he was reluctant to sell it.

He mumbled and stammered and even denied ever knowing a Mr. Smith; but after an hour or so he broke down and said: "So waddya want?"

"I want to buy your car," I said, playing hard to get.
He explained that I didn't need to know his address because the little old lady from Pasadena lived in his house and it would break her heart if she saw me drive off in it.

Well, finally he said we should meet at a deserted, weed strewn parking lot behind an abandoned opium den and not to tell anyone. This sounded really promising; especially when he said I couldn't miss it because there were no occupied buildings within a mile radius of the place.

It took me a while to get there but when I saw the little beauty I knew it was a car worth the struggle.

The dignity with which her sleek lines were accentuated by the garbage and rubble on which she was unevenly balanced was heartwarming. She was sheathed in a non-reflective mysterious gray paint lovingly applied by a caring person with a trowel.

The unknown artisan had been so enthusiastic that half the windshield was covered in his gray artistry. But, as the owner pointed out, "Hey, what's the big deal man, it's on the passenger side innit?" He had obviously guessed that I was nobody's fool.

Clearly the owner was nervous and very upset at having to part with his pride and joy. He paced back and forth on the rubble kicking half bricks with his steel toed loafers, twitching and glancing over his shoulder so that I could hardly see his face.

And that silly old ski mask didn't help either. Obviously he didn't realize that it would make it difficult to recognize him if we ever met at a social gathering and I wanted to introduce him to the chief of police.

Anyway, I was pleased to see the front bumper dangling gracefully from a piece of good quality wire. I'm too wise to fall for the old "bad quality piece of wire" trick. But as I sauntered slowly around the vehicle intending to kick the tires he kept leaping in front of each wheel not seeming to mind being repeatedly kicked in the shins.

It was time to assert myself. "I would like to kick the tires" I said.

"Why?" was his terse rejoinder as he adjusted his ski mask.

"Because I don't really wish to know the condition of your shins" My sarcasm was lost on him just as his assurance that the tires were just fine was lost on me.

Well, it turned out he was right; the tires were nice and shiny. And I'm ashamed to say I was insensitive enough to call them bald. "Why in the world would you want hairy tires he chuckled?" Well, there really was no answer to that. He said he was beginning to wonder if I was smart enough to appreciate the fact that there was no passenger seat to add weight and make the car slower.

Well, I can tell you, I was glad I hadn't complained that the back seats were also missing. That would really have made me look silly.

As soon as I handed over my hundred dollars he was gone. Obviously he was sensitive and couldn't bear the pain of lengthy good-byes.

It didn't take more than a couple of hours to start the engine and when I arrived home I could see I was the envy of the street because all my neighbors came out to stare in wonderment, pointing and laughing and dancing little jigs.

My girl friend was the one who looked the most surprised. She seemed to be in quite a daze as she swung the starting handle over and over until the engine roared into life; and as we were lucky enough to have no passenger seats she was delighted to sit on the bare steel floor and nurse her starting handle blisters.

But this was just the beginning of the fun. As we chugged merrily along, black exhaust smoke poured through the floor and all the vents, and although it was difficult to see through the windshield it was also very romantic.

We each knew the other was there because of the choking coughs; and my girl friend was smart enough to hold the gear stick in place after each gear change to prevent it shooting back into neutral with a loud thump.

I'm sure she was pleased to have something to do - especially as she was down there with the gearshift anyway.

We would reach out blindly and poke each other playfully in the eye to show affection. Of course I couldn't see her but I made an effort to remember she was sitting on the floor.

Sometimes, I wonder what happened to her. I never saw her again after that wonderful day. Perhaps the silly thing couldn't keep up with the high life.

44. WHAT'S YOUR POSITION
ON COUCH POTATOES?

If you think that Feng Shui is a Chinese restaurant then you are probably living in a building that is the wrong shape with all your furniture facing the wrong way.

Feng Shui, you see, is the 4000 year old Chinese art of geomancy, which advocates placing beds and desks and stuff in the best position to produce harmonious vibes.

It also helps if you want a cup of tea in a hurry.
In pre-Feng Shui days, kitchen sink taps were sometimes positioned upside down. This did not make for good vibes – especially when you wanted to fill the kettle. Anyway, now you know why people were always walking 10 miles through snowdrifts to the nearest well.

These pre-Geomancy inconveniences also applied to all the bathroom fittings. I am sure your imagination will save me a whole paragraph of colorful, descriptive narrative that will only be edited.

Learning about the power of Feng Shui has helped me better understand all the stuff that went wrong in our house when I was a kid. I'm pretty sure that if my dad had known about the benefits of Geomancy he would have made our recalcitrant dog sit facing the therapeutic baseball bat where he could see what was coming.

The furniture would certainly have been safer from his arbitrary choices of suitable restroom facilities. (No, not my dad's, the dog's)

Our coffee table would probably have produced more Feng Shui domestic harmony if it were placed behind the couch where we couldn't see what the dog was doing to it. But the darned table took root because it figured that if the dog were going to treat it like a tree, it might as well be one.

Young people will wonder why we needed a couch at all when there was no television. Well, you see, even in those days we had couch potatoes to help make us feel self- righteous just for standing up and scratching.

Maybe you don't know this, but couch potatoes are able to operate fairly efficiently even without the prop of a television. It's their nature. All they require is an absence of anything that threatens to be intellectually stimulating. Sure, television is best but not essential.

It was really scary to watch our dad sitting there staring at the wall for hours - especially when he said something intellectual like, "shut up," if we interrupted whatever he was staring at.

The funny thing is that if you were to follow Feng Shui principles today, the harmonious position of the couch could well turn out to be in a different room than the harmonious position of the television.

This could easily upset your dad's vibes. You would do well to keep him away from the therapeutic baseball bat when there was racing on the television and he was stuck in the next room with just the harmonious couch for company – which could sometimes turn out to be faster than the horses he bet on. But, at least, in those days we were adept at the art of conversation:

"Tell me, Dad, why do you sit watching a wall?"

"Son, I'm not in a position to tell you that."

"Well, dad, why don't you just change your position?"

"Son, right now I'm leaning toward making your face more harmonious."

Then I would have been made to stand in the wrong corner and mess up my vibes for a week.

Of course, later I could cheer myself up by messing with the Feng Shui of the bathroom - which would mess up everyone's vibes.

The possibilities of Feng Shui are endless. Who knows, one day our leaders might decide that the Amazon jungle would be more harmonious if the trees were integrated with oil derricks. Like, ten trees down and one derrick up, right?

The problem with this idea is that when today's kids become the tax paying workers of America, they will inherit the benefits of the national debt, right? Well, you never know with kids, they may be ungrateful enough to wish that we had been shipped to the Amazon, too.

Just the same, it's our duty to arrange for the proper positioning of our progeny. And it's their duty to keep paying our harmonious social security benefits. That's my position, anyway.

So this means that... Oh, what the heck, why don't we just go to a Chinese restaurant, instead?

45. ECOLOGICAL DILEMMA

The world is teeming with endangered species. They are everywhere - eating each other. Maybe this is why they are endangered. You're right; enough with the cynicism, let's get positive.

The thing is, we all have our favorite species, which we insist should be allowed to survive at the expense of the food chain link just below them.

In some places the gray wolf has been removed from the endangered species list and relegated to merely threatened, which means that the link below them is now endangered. Ok, wolves eat Elk and Buffalo. It's only natural, right?

But what about Elk lovers and Buffalo buffs? After all, their favorite species eats only grass? Seems harmless but, all kinds of things live in grass. If the Elk and Buffalo are not stopped, what will Grasshoppers hop in?

The Mexican gray wolf retains its current status as endangered. This is because there are now only 22 of the little critters left. And to help them catch an occasional buffalo while competing with 20,000 merely threatened gray wolves, they will be allowed American drivers licenses. But only until they become merely threatened, then they will have to walk like everybody else.

So we are on the horns of an ecological dilemma, are we not? And since it's been left to me to come up with a scientific solution, my suggestion is that we put "cute" at the top of the list. Everybody loves "cute."

The answer has got to be frogs. As long ago as 1998, Scientists gathered at Hamline University Campus, Minnesota, to discuss issues of the declining frog population. Some blamed it on pollution.

Researchers warned that the only frogs that will remain in the future might be virtual frogs, concrete lawn frogs and frog jewelry. This is a threat, right?

But we have another dilemma. Frogs eat insects. That's as it should be, you might say. But it's unlikely that the insect lobby will see it that way. How long before we get a list that includes endangered dung beetles and fragile fruit flies and a suggestion that we label them so that the endangered frog will know not to eat them?

Of course, this dilemma stretches far beyond the shores of America. The French, who don't care about dung beetles, are very fond of frogs and snails. They even have a pet name for them: Dinner.

After the Minnesota report, the French are concerned that they will soon be left with only "virtual dinner". This means the animals most likely to become endangered species in France are all those that kill frogs and snails.

It goes without saying that snails, though they are not at the bottom of the food chain, are certainly the slowest. This can be a hindrance to survival when you're being chased by an eagle. So a meeting of the Save Our French Snails Society was convened, where a rheumy-eyed individual took another sip of Burgundy and slurred something about supplying the snails with tiny motorbikes.

Luckily, saner minds prevailed and pointed out that snail motorbikes would cause pollution which kills frogs and... Well, nobody said saving the world would be easy.

But to get back to the bigger stuff like wolves and mountain lions. Well, after careful consideration, I've decided that the best solution is to gather all the animals in one place and teach them to love each other and not just each other's flavor.

Someone (not me) will volunteer to stand bravely in the middle of the group and insist that they all become vegetarians, forthwith. There must be rules. The wolves and elk must learn to get along peacefully, and love each other just as humans do.

Anybody who eats someone will be sent to a counselor for therapy. This would, admittedly, be cruel and unusual.

We all know, very well that most of them would rather be eaten. Ok, I realize this idea is not as scientific as motorbikes for frogs, but, at least it won't affect the ecology – well, not much anyway.

I wasn't going to mention the 18 endangered Arizona Pygmy owls. But I've just learned that the Bush administration is going to take them off the endangered list. All 18 of them.

Of course, this makes perfect sense if the, "save the mouse society" paid more into the election fund than the, "protect the owl society." And politics is, after all, dog eat dog – or whatever happens to be the lowest link in the food chain, right?

46. CHRISTMAS CHEER

Remember when you were little you wanted Christmas to come quickly? It always took forever, didn't it? You used to wonder why on earth Christmas couldn't come as quickly as bedtime did.

161

Well, you got your wish didn't you? Now it seems like Christmas comes every ten minutes. It's too darned late to be careful what you wish for now; you've done it, so just try to be jolly or something, OK?

Anyway Santa is back in the Mall again, and there's nothing you can do about it. And no, my middle name is not Scrooge. It's... Ok, it's Ebenezer.

Yes. I know that kids love Santa. And, why not? Santa brings gifts for everyone in the world and never gets any himself. The jolly old guy sits in the Mall and promises kids' motorbikes and nuclear submarines and he's always sooo happy.

Well, let's face it, wouldn't you be happy if you could promise someone else's kids whatever you like. "Sure kid, whatever you like, I'll bring it, trust me." Yeah, right.

I mean, it's no skin off Santa's nose, is it? He'll be back at the North Pole before the kid starts howling and you have to get creative. "Where's my nuclear submarine? Where is it? Where is it? Oh, I see, it's a nuclear Barbie. Ok, thanks mom."

When I was a kid we didn't have Malls. We had to have faith. We had to believe in Santa on trust. "You better believe in Santa, you little lout," my mother used to say, patting me on the head with the Christmas tree. "Or Santa won't bring you your father's old long johns or your brother's half used toe fungus ointment for Christmas.

But I was better off than the baby. She always got a bottle of after shave lotion from dad and a plug of chewing tobacco from grandma.

The only reason they brought Santa into it at all was because they needed someone to blame for the gifts. Naturally, it was scary for a kid not to believe in Santa. I mean, imagine having to go through another year without half used toe fungus ointment. You can't can you?

And then there was Santa's milk and cookies. I used to spend hours trying to figure that out. Why would Santa want my milk and cookies? Why can't he being his own milk and cookies? Seems like extortion to me. "Hey, kid, no cookies, no long johns, ok?" Some role model.

Get yourself a red suit and a sack and you can steal kids' cookies. And coming down the chimney is not even breaking and entering. It's just entering, right?

One good thing about old time Christmas is that our dad wanted us to be bad all year. This is because we needed the coal for the fire. "Listen, you little oaf, if you're good one more time you're grounded. And he would send me to his room. This is because his room was even scarier than mine, but we won't go there right now.

Of course, the observance of Christmas is always changing. In Charles Dickens' day there was lot's of snow. And Santa never brought any coal – even if the whole family was bad – and there were work houses and kids on crutches with no turkey. Ah, the good old days.

The reason my dad never had much success as Santa was because his heart wasn't really in it. I mean, he thought scrooge was the hero, for heaven's sake.

I guess it's easy to make this mistake when Scrooge is the only one in the story who ends up handing out turkeys and puckering up for a thank you kiss under the mistletoe.

Ok, some of the benefactors preferred to forget the mistletoe bit and give back the turkey, but it's the thought that counts, isn't it?

So there you are. I hope I've contributed to the Christmas spirit. And, remember, if you need a Santa for Christmas, I've got plenty of toe fungus ointment and long johns and if that doesn't make the kids happy, I don't know what will, the little... Anyway, Merry Christmas.

Printed in the United Kingdom
by Lightning Source UK Ltd.
106454UKS00095B/125